NEW YEAR'S FAYE

DOGG PACK
BOOK 6

EVIE MITCHELL

THUNDER THIGHS PUBLISHING

Cover design and illustrations by Laras Putri
Editing by Emerald Edits and Evermore Edits

Special thanks to the three expert / sensitivity readers who contributed their time and effort to this book.

ACKNOWLEDGEMENT OF COUNTRY

I acknowledge the Traditional Custodians of the lands on which I write, the Ngunnawal people, and pay my respect to elders both past and present.

I acknowledge the continued and deep spiritual relationship of all Australian Aboriginal and Torres Strait Islander peoples' to this land, and their unique cultural and spiritual relationships to the land, waters and seas and their rich contribution to society.

BLURB

Faye's New Year's Resolution
  1. Eat a piece of fruit
  2. Exercise more
  3. Reduce stress
  4. Annul accidental marriage to Sam Dogg

When I woke on New Year's Day married to Sam Dogg—my friend, boss, and lead guitarist of The Wild Ones—I did what I do best, I made a list and took control of the situation.

The solution? Stay married until the end of the band's world tour, then quietly get an annulment. Simple, professional, perfectly planned.

Except Sam's not exactly cooperating... and neither is my heart.

Sam's New Year's Resolution
1. Happily Ever After with Faye

1

FAYE

FROM THE DESK OF FAYE MOYO,
PUBLIC RELATIONS MANGER FOR THE
WILD ONES

TO DO LIST: NEW YEAR'S EVE
PERFORMANCE

Priority Level: CRITICAL
Status: IN PROGRESS

- ~~Double-check sound equipment (completed 4pm)~~

- ~~Review security protocols with venue (completed 5pm)~~
- ~~Final wardrobe checks for band (completed 6pm)~~
- Ensure Justice stays AWAY from the tequila pre-show (barely achieved)
- Coordinate timing with pyrotechnics team
- Monitor social media response
- Remember to breathe

Note: Everything is under control. Everything is fine.

Secondary Note: Stop making lists about breathing!!

CONTINGENCY PLANS
A) Technical difficulties
B) Weather issues
C) Fan incidents
D) Justice finding the tequila

Current Status: T-minus 10 minutes to midnight
Threat Level: Manageable

Personal Note: Stop touching your dress. It's <u>fine!</u>

~

I smoothed down my red dress for the hundredth time, scanning the packed venue from my position in the wings of the stage. The Wild Ones had the crowd eating from their hands—as if there'd been any doubt. Energy pulsed through the room like a living beast, tingling your skin and making your heart race, whipping the crowd into a frenzy as the clock counted down to the new year.

Chars, the heart of Astipia, transformed for New Year's Eve. The stage was set up right in front of the palace, with glittering high-rises and historic brick buildings looming around us like silent witnesses, their windows glowing faintly in the winter night. It had that familiar, exhilarating bustle you might find in London, where history and modernity collided in a rush of light and energy.

Overhead, strings of lights crisscrossed the streets, hanging from lampposts and building facades, bathing everything in a warm, golden glow that contrasted sharply with the icy breeze. Snow had dusted the city earlier, and now remnants clung stubbornly to the sidewalks, crunching into slush underfoot. The winter air held a sharpness that seeped through even the thickest coat, but no one seemed to mind. Not tonight. Tonight, the cold was just part of the magic.

The Wild Ones owned the stage, each of them seeming larger than life against the vast, glittering city backdrop. The crowd was a living, breathing mass, bundled in coats, scarves, and hats, but still moving, swaying, reaching toward the band as if trying to grab onto the last notes of the song that throbbed through the speakers. The energy was palpable, a crackling, pulsing force, the crowd feral as the clock counted down to midnight.

Nine minutes and thirteen seconds to go.

Justice's voice rose and fell with the perfect blend of raw edge and polished charm, like he knew exactly which notes would crawl under your skin and stay there. The opening chords of the band's newest single, "Midnight Kiss", echoed through the arena, making every heartbeat in the crowd sync with the pulsing bass. The irony of the song's title wasn't lost on me—especially not as I stood in the shadows at the edge of the stage, watching Justice work his magic. A dozen women in the front row were utterly transfixed, eyes wide, mouths parted, leaning toward him as though he might pull them into his orbit with a single glance.

Each one looked like they were desperate to be his midnight kiss.

He looked every bit the rock star tonight, the soft glow of the stage lights casting shadows along the sharp angles of his face. His black suit clung to him, tailored perfectly to his lean frame, though he'd discarded his jacket halfway through the set, tossing it into the sea of hands reaching for him. His dark dress shirt was unbuttoned just enough to hint at the tattoos peeking out from beneath.

Radley caught my eye from behind her drum kit as she launched into a solo that was as fierce and unpredictable as she was. She tossed me a wink, her curls—once neatly arranged; now wild and untamed—framing her face as she poured herself into each beat. Her body moved with the music, like she and the drums were one entity, driving the energy in the room higher and higher.

And then there was Felix. The red-haired bassist played his guitar with the smoothness of a man twice his age. His bass lines slithered through the air, low and seductive, a current beneath the melody that you could feel in your bones. The steady, deep hum of the bass wrapped around the audience until they weren't just listening to the music—they were part of it, lost somewhere between the thrill of the performance and the ache of watching someone you can't quite reach.

But it was Sam who drew my gaze like a magnet.

He moved across the stage like he was born to be there, each step and gesture effortless yet purposeful, his fingers dancing over the guitar strings with a feverish intensity. His hands moved so fast, it was as if they were possessed by some otherworldly force, channeling something raw and electric with each note. His bow tie, once neat at the start of the show, now hung loosely around his neck, a forgotten relic of formality in the heat of his performance. The collar of his crisp white dress shirt revealled a hint of his lean muscles, the fabric clinging to his shoulders and chest in the hot glow of the stage lights—a contrast to the cold winter nights air.

Under the spotlights, he seemed to glow, a halo of golden light casting shadows along the contours of his jaw and the high cheekbones that only seemed sharper under the intensity of his concentration. He closed his eyes, and it was like he let go of something, sinking deeper into the music. The slight furrow in his brow softened, replaced by an expression of pure, unguarded passion.

He bent his head, and his dark-brown hair fell forward, tumbling across his forehead in a way that I knew would drive his fans wild.

There were social media pages dedicated to his fringe.

I lifted my phone, snapping off pictures for their socials. As their marketing and public relations manager, it was my job to make them look good twenty-four seven. And even though it was New Year's Eve, this was one of our biggest events of the entire year—which meant that my job wouldn't be done until they were all safely tucked in their beds.

I panned to the crowd, capturing their ecstatic energy.

Nights like this made the sacrifice worthwhile.

"Five minutes to countdown!" Liz, my assistant, chirped through my earpiece. "Everyone in position?"

I tapped my mic. "Copy that. Main stage is secured."

The band closed out their next song and the lights blinked out, bathing the stage in darkness. I blinked rapidly, watching as the band reset, getting ready for their final song.

This one had to be timed perfectly, and the

clock at the front of the stage was the watch by which we lived and died tonight. There could be no mistakes.

"Two minutes!"

I grabbed my mobile phone, preparing to ring in the new year with a livestream for their social media from my safe position in the wings.

The opening notes rang out—a raw, gritty guitar riff from Sam that sliced through the silence and sent the audience into a frenzy. He dragged the sound out, letting it reverberate through the speakers, each note hitting like a pulse, thrumming through the floor and into my chest.

The bass kicked in next Felix's deep, rolling line that seemed to come from somewhere primal, anchoring the wild energy of the song. Then Radley's drums exploded like thunder the stage lights flashing in time with her beat— relentless, and somehow a little chaotic, matching the song's name and spirit. The crowd, already loud, erupted, their screams almost drowning out the music.

Justice stepped forward, owning the stage. His voice, dark and rich, poured into the mic, filling the space with a raspy intensity.

"Wild Heart" was the band's anthem, their first big hit and the one that had turned them into legends. The lyrics were rough and unapologetic, a love letter to every risk they'd ever taken, every rule they'd ever broken. Justice didn't just sing it; he *lived* it, pouring every ounce of himself into each line.

"I was born in the dark, made for the fight,
Running on heart and a devil's light.
Broke all the rules, lost my way,
But I'd rather burn out than fade away."

The words cut through the roar of the crowd, drawing the audience in. Justice leaned forward, one hand gripping the mic stand, his other hand reaching out as if he were pulling them into his world. I could hear the screaming of fans as they sang along with him, their voices blending with his in a harmony that thrilled me.

"Wild heart, I can't be chained,
Fire in my blood, lightning in my veins.
I'll break the walls, I'll tear apart,
I'm a storm, I'm a spark, I'm a wild heart."

The song built and built, each verse more intense than the last.

I stood in the wings, delighted to capture this moment on camera—already knowing this would be a key feature for our social media campaign over the next few weeks.

But Sam, apparently, had other ideas.

He caught my eye mid-solo, a dangerous grin spreading across his face. I knew that look. That was his I'm-about-to-cause-chaos look.

I narrowed my eyes at him in warning.

"One minute!"

The final countdown began, voices rising in anticipation. Sam stepped back from his mic, still playing but now moving with purpose toward my side of the stage.

Toward me.

"Thirty seconds!"

"Oh hell no," I mouthed at him, glaring with the fire of a thousands suns.

"Twenty seconds!"

He reached the edge of the stage, still playing, still grinning like the devil himself.

"Fifteen seconds!"

In one smooth motion, he pulled the guitar strap over his head, passing the instrument to a waiting stage tech without missing a beat.

"Ten!"

He caught my hand, ignoring my squeak of protest.

"Nine!"

"Eight!"

He pulled me onto the stage.

"Seven!"

"Six!"

He pushed me toward Justice, accepting his guitar back with a seamless transition from the trailing tech. Justice wrapped an arm around my neck, holding me in place between them as they both leaned forward, screaming the final lines into the microphone.

"*I'll break the walls, I'll tear apart,*"

"Five!"

"Four!"

"Three!"

"*I'm a storm, I'm a spark, I'm a wild heart!*"

"Two!"

Sam struck a final chord on his guitar as the lights all around us went black.

"ONE!"

The crowd erupted as fireworks burst from behind the stage, shooting into the midnight sky. The light show bathed everyone in streams of gold and silver, as confetti and streamers exploded from the front of the stage, covering the laughing, kissing, celebrating crowd in shimmering paper.

Sam's warm hand caught mine, tugging me close. His soft lips gently brushed my cheek, completely at odds with the heaving chaos surrounding us.

"Happy New Year, Faye," he murmured, his breath tickling my ear.

My heart skipped, fluttering with a mix of nostalgia and something softer, sweeter, almost unreal—like we were reliving an old memory that had never happened but somehow felt inevitable. I closed my eyes, dizzy with the thrill of a perfect show, a closing chapter, a new year of possibilities.

I leaned into him enjoying the fireworks show. "Happy New Year, you annoying pest."

His chuckle was lost as Justice launched into "Auld Lang Syne," with the crowd quickly joining in. Felix and Radley fell in, providing the instrumental backing. I stepped back as Sam let me go, adding his guitar to the mix.

Justice wrapped an arm around me, thrusting the microphone into my face. With a laugh, I shoved it away but let him pull me close as we sang.

Their set wrapped a few songs later as I quickly uploaded some footage to their socials and hit send on their pre-recorded New Year's message.

"Faye! Put down the phone!" Radley ordered, wrapping one sweaty arm around my shoulders and carrying me along with them as they tumbled through the backstage area. "It's New Year's Day!"

"Just one more—"

She plucked the phone out of my hand, tucking it into her bra. "Try me."

I snorted, hip-bumping her. "Babe, if you

think that's gonna stop me you have another think coming."

We walked down and into the churning crowd, being swept along with the revelers as security kept us safe.

I hunched my shoulders, pulling my coat tighter around me, grateful I'd thought to grab it before leaving the warmth of the stage. Winter had settled over the city around us, biting and unforgiving—but beautiful. My breath fogged faintly as we moved through the crowd, stopping here and there for the band to sign autographs and take pictures.

Around us, the remnants of New Year's celebrations hung on snow-dusted buildings mixed in with forgotten pieces of mistletoe and Christmas lights, and the occasional menorah in a window.

We followed security around to the back of the stage, weaving through the tight area and out onto a back alley.

"Shots!" Justice held up the bottle of tequila he'd pulled from God only knew where. "Come on, Faye." He shook it enticingly. "You've orchestrated the perfect show, the perfect countdown, the perfect everything. Time to let loose!"

"Leave her alone," Sam said, but I could

hear the smile in his voice. "You know Faye doesn't do unplanned fun."

I glanced back at him, poking my tongue out. "I do too!"

The entire band turned to look at me with identical expressions of disbelief.

"Name one time," Radley challenged with a laugh. "I dare you."

"I..." My mind raced through five years of touring, searching for a single moment of spontaneity.

"The time she let us order pizza without checking Yelp reviews first?" Felix offered.

"And because of that we all ended up with food poisoning," Justice countered.

Sam's chest rumbled with laughter behind me. "Face it, babe. You're about as spontaneous as a tax return."

There had to be something in the air, because unlike the other million times Sam had teased me, this time the way *"babe"* rolled off his tongue so casually, made my spine tingle even as I grounded my teeth together at his stupid dig.

It shouldn't hurt that people assumed I wasn't fun. I was! Just because I had structured, planned times to let loose didn't make it any less fun.

Tax return. I'll how him how spontaneous I can be.

"Fine." I straightened, squaring my shoulders. "One shot." I held up a finger. "One."

Justice's eyes widened. "Wait, really?"

"Really." I grabbed the bottle from his hands, determined to prove them all wrong. "But I'm instigating our responsible drinking protocols."

The band groaned in unison.

"Faye..." Justice pouted. "Really?"

"It's practical. Item one: establish a designated driver—"

"Already handled," Radley cut in. "Car service is booked until noon tomorrow."

"Item two: ensure proper hydration—"

"Got water bottles in the car and the hotel rooms," Felix said.

"Item three: maintain professional boundaries—"

Radley squeezed my shoulders and leaned in, licking my cheek. "Like this?"

"Radley!"

She laughed, dancing away.

I looked at the shot glass Justice held out, tempted to take it but also strangely terrified.

Well, not so strangely if I allowed myself to remember why I instigated a no drinking policy in the first place.

Alex.

The remnant shadow and humiliation and shame burned the back of my throat as I stared at the glass.

My ex-boyfriend had taken me out drinking the night before a big presentation. We'd worked at the same firm, keeping our relationship secret. I'd thought it romantic and taboo—never realizing that the only reason he'd wanted in my pants was to steal my ideas.

He'd gotten me wasted, left me at home to sleep it off, then presented my ideas as his own to the client thus winning the account that should have been mine. As a result, I'd been seen as flaky and unreliable.

I'd lost my job a few months later.

"Come on, Faye." Sam's warm breath brushed the shell of my ear. "Don't let him steal more of your joy. You can do this."

I took the shot glass.

"To The Wild Ones," I said, raising it high. "And to..." I hesitated.

"To unplanned moments," Sam said, wrapping an arm around my shoulders. "And memories we'll never forget."

"To the memories!" the band echoed.

I blanched, shooting Sam a look when he chuckled at my discomfort.

The tequila warmed my blood as the party

kicked into full swing. We made our way through the streets to a small dive bar the band had rented out for those who had worked on the concert. Our roadies and crew poured into the tiny venue, taking advantage of the free food and booze on offer.

I squeezed myself into a minuscule booth with Sam, laughing as Justice commandeered the sound system, turning our private afterparty into what he called a "proper celebration."

"Ten bucks says he tries to stage dive onto one of the couches within the hour," Sam murmured, pouring me a glass of water.

I accepted it gratefully. "Twenty says he tries to convince Radley to let him crowd surf on the cleaning crew first."

Sam's laugh rumbled deep in his chest. "This is why you're my favorite."

A warm tingle raced down my spine to pool in my belly at his words. A spark of something igniting as our thighs brushed.

That is the tequila talking.

I cleared my throat, forcing myself to tease him back. "Because I enable your gambling habit?"

"Because you know our boy better than he knows himself." He nudged my shoulder with his. "Speaking of which..."

I followed his gaze to where Justice was climbing onto a chair, shirt already missing.

"I got it." I moved out of the booth, straightening my dress as I put my game face on. "Justice! What's our rule about staying clothed at industry events?"

"But it's just us!" He wobbled precariously.

"And the cleanup crew, three security guards, roadies, and—" I squinted at the corner. "—is that the venue owner's daughter recording this?"

Justice's eyes widened as he scrambled down.

Sam's familiar chuckle hit my ear as his hand pressed against my lower back. He leaned down to whisper in my ear, "And that's why you're the real rock star here."

"Hardly." But I leaned into his touch, just slightly. Just enough. "Someone has to keep you lot from trending for the wrong reasons."

"Hey, my trends are always tasteful."

I arched an eyebrow at him. "The Great Pants Incident of 2019?"

"That was one time!"

"The Dolphin Debacle?"

"Those charges were dropped."

"The Valentine's Day—"

His hand slid around my waist, spinning me

to face the makeshift dance floor where Felix was attempting to teach Radley some TikTok dance. "Dance with me instead of listing my crimes?"

"That's not a denial," I pointed out, but let him pull me closer as the music shifted to something slower.

"Never said it was." His other hand found mine, warm and calloused from guitar strings. "Just trying to distract you before you remember the Coffee Shop Crisis."

"The Coffee Shop—" I blanched. "Samuel Dogg, you promised we'd never speak of that again."

His grin was wicked. "Dance with me and I'll keep your secret about the barista and the whipped cream."

"You wouldn't *dare*."

"Try me." But his eyes were soft, teasing.

This was our dance, our rhythm. Push and pull, tease and protect, always knowing exactly where the lines were.

Sure, there might be the seed of attraction there; I mean what person wouldn't find a cute rock star attractive?

But I'd never let it take root. Sam mattered too much to me as both a friend and client.

But one dance couldn't hurt.

I relaxed into his hold, letting him sway us

gently. "Fine. But only because I'm protecting your reputation."

"Of course." His thumb brushed over my knuckles. "Nothing to do with how much you love dancing with me."

"You're not that special, Dogg."

"No?" He spun me out, then back into his chest with practiced ease. "Name one other person who knows exactly how you take your coffee after dealing with Justice's pranks."

"Extra hot, double shot—"

"Triple shot," he corrected. "Extra hot, triple shot, with a splash of vanilla but only if it's before noon. After noon it's straight espresso because you say the vanilla makes you too soft for negotiations."

Warmth that had nothing to do with tequila spread through my chest. "Lucky guess."

"Just like I'm guessing you've got at least three contingency plans for Justice's inevitable attempt to recreate the New Year's ball drop using the chandelier?"

I bit my lip. "Four, actually."

His laugh vibrated through me, and for just a moment, I allowed myself to sink against him, resting my weight against his length.

How nice it would be to have something—or someone—like Sam in my—

"Faye! Emergency!" Felix's voice shattered

the moment. "Justice found the pyrotechnics control panel!"

I stepped back, professional mask sliding into place. "Duty calls."

Sam's hand lingered on my waist for a heartbeat longer than necessary. "Go save the day, PR Queen. I'll make sure the fire extinguishers are ready."

"Our regular Tuesday night then?"

His smile softened. "Wouldn't have it any other way."

I hurried off to prevent Justice from recreating the Fourth of July indoors, trying to ignore how cold my skin felt where Sam's hands had been; trying even harder to ignore how right it had felt to be in his arms.

Professional boundaries, I reminded myself firmly. I'd learned that lesson the hard way with Alex.

But as Sam's laugh echoed across the room, warm and familiar as a favorite song, I wondered if maybe some boundaries were meant to be crossed.

Just not tonight.

"Justice Wilder, put down that lighter right now!"

2

FAYE

HANGOVER & SITUATION ASSESSMENT

Priority Level: CRITICAL
Status: DISASTER IN PROGRESS

CURRENT SYMPTOMS:
- ☐ Headache: SEVERE
- ☐ Nausea: Increasing
- ☐ Memory: Fragmented
- ☐ Dignity: Missing in action

IMMEDIATE CONCERNS:
- ☐ Unknown person in bed
- ☐ Strange ring on finger
- ☐ Still wearing last night's dress
- ☐ Smell like a distillery

```
CONTINGENCY PLANS
A) Quiet escape
B) Fake own death
C) Move to different country
D) NEVER drink tequila again
(Blame Justice)


Current Status: One (1) massive
life crisis
Threat Level: APOCALYPTIC


Personal Note: Stop panicking.
There has to be a logical
explanation.


Secondary Note: Why does the other
person's breathing sound familiar?


Final Note: Oh God, is that Sam?
```

~

The pounding in my head alerted me to the fact I *may* have overindulged the night before.

May? Girl, you got wasted.

Vague images of Radley, Felix, and Justice plying me with alcohol floated through my head. There'd been shots at the bar followed by terrible karaoke, a greasy kebab on a sidewalk, then… something to do with drumsticks??? It all became a bit blurry after that.

I gingerly opened one eye to assess the damage.

Light sensitivity, hammering headache, nauseous stomach, still dressed in my fabulous gown from last night while smelling like a gin factory.

I huffed out a soft groan.

Yep. All evidence indicates I partied like it was 1999.

I screwed my eye closed and reached blindly for the blanket, hauling it up and over my head. I curled my legs into my chest and slid my hands under my cheek only to jerk back when something sharp scrapped my jaw.

Rubbing one hand over the other I found the offensive item.

"What the fuck?" Jerking upright, I tossed the blanket off, and stared at the *GIANT FREAKING ROCK* on my ring finger.

"Oh no. Oh no, no, no, no, no!"

A moan came from the other side of the bed.

Squealing in fright, I rolled off the mattress to land with a thump on the floor of the hotel room.

Springing back up, I snatched the only item

within reach, brandishing it as I waited for the stranger to emerge from under the blankets.

"Who are you and why are you in my room?" I barked, waving my bright-pink vibrator from side to side. "Show yourself!"

"Faye?" A horrifyingly familiar, deliciously sexy voice growled from under the blankets. "It's me. Now be quiet and come back to bed unless you're planning on ordering a shit-ton of room service and painkillers."

The vibrator fell limply from my hands, my mouth opening and shutting as I struggled to process the reality of our current predicament.

"Sam?"

My boss pulled the blankets down, squinting up at me through bloodshot eyes. His dark-brown hair stood at strange angles, while his white dress shirt lay open at his throat to reveal a swath of tan skin that remained sun-kissed despite it being mid-winter.

A present from the sperm donor he'd never met, he'd once told me with a wry laugh before changing the subject.

"What?" He scrubbed a hand over his slightly green face. In the quiet of the room, I could hear his palm rasp against the scruff of his beard.

I swallowed, fighting a wave of nausea. "Are you, by any chance, wearing a wedding ring?"

Please say no. Please say no. Please say—

He blinked twice, then pulled his left arm from under the bedsheets, thrusting his hand forward.

"Oh," he murmured, staring at the ring glinting in the warm morning light. "Shit."

And with that, the floor rushed up to meet me.

"SPENDING NEW YEAR'S Day in a hospital with you wasn't on my bingo card for this year," Sam said dryly as he scrolled through his phone from his seat beside my hospital bed.

"Yeah well, people should learn to create bedside tables that don't permanently injure you." I lifted the icepack from my head. "Is it bad?"

He glanced up from his scroll, his dark-brown eyes narrowing as he assessed my injury. He stood, leaning across the bed. His hand lifted as if to touch me, his eyes soft and assessing. My breath caught as he swept his knuckles over my cheek in a surprisingly tender move.

My heart felt shaky and unsettled. There was a new dynamic between us thanks to the rings on our fingers. But his care when I'd found myself bleeding and disorientated, his gentle, reassuring touches each time I'd been unsure were throwing me off-balance.

I didn't like that I liked it.

"Not at all," Sam said finally, lying sweetly but outing himself with a poorly concealed wince.

The man had no poker face.

I groaned, slapping the icepack back on my bump. "And just before the tour too."

Sam snorted. "As if that's your main concern."

Damn him, he knew exactly what worried me—the paparazzi.

News of our whirlwind marriage had spread like wildfire. My phone vibrated every 0.2 seconds with some new notification, no doubt most of them coming from my parents demanding to know what the fuck had happened.

You tell me.

It seemed drunk Faye and drunk Sam had decided that getting married at 4am on New Year's Day was a great idea.

I'll note that I was apparently drunk enough to get married, but sober enough to remember to wear my silk bonnet to bed.

Priorities, am I right?

I glanced back at Sam, taking in his profile

as he resumed scrolling through his phone, assessing the damage.

He still wore his black dress pants and crisp white shirt from the night before, sans jacket and bow tie, and plus a shit-ton of wrinkles. He'd tossed a leather jacket over his ensemble as I'd been hustled into an ambulance by some friendly but starstruck paramedics.

I guess it wasn't every day they were called to the room of a rock star to deal with the head injury of his PR manager.

And, apparently, wife.

I gulped.

"Oh look, we've made the *Chars Times*," Sam chuckled. "Damn. That's a good picture."

He held up the phone for my perusal and—sure enough—there we stood in technicolored fabulousness.

Someone must have snapped the photo at last night's New Year's Eve gig. I wore the gorgeous floor-length red gown that hugged every one of my curves. The shade of the dress, coupled with a light touch of shimmering blush, had made my dark-brown skin glow. Whoever said dark red and melanin didn't go together was obviously tripping. Sam looked quite dapper in his black tuxedo, complete with a jaunty bow tie. The picture had to have been taken sometime before midnight as we'd partied, prior to ringing in the new year with the epic gig we'd worked all year to secure.

The words began to swirl on the screen. Swallowing against a sudden bout of nausea, I handed him back his cell. "Read it to me."

"*Samuel Dogg, twenty-eight and lead guitarist of The Wild Ones.*" He glanced up and pointed to himself. "—That's me."

I suppressed a smile. "Noted."

"*Has rung in the new year in surprising fashion. Sources from the Little Chapel in Chars have confirmed that the superstar has married hometown friend and the band's publicist, Faye Moyo.*" He pointed at me. "That's you."

A grin tugged at my lips. "I had no idea."

"*Moyo, twenty-seven, has been with the band for five years following her graduation from Ravenburn College with a degree in Marketing and Public Relations.*" Sam cocked one eyebrow. "Has it really been five years?"

"If they printed it in the paper, it must be true."

"*It is the first marriage for both Dogg and Moyo, who share a close working relationship.*" He frowned. "It *is* your first marriage, right?"

"As far as I'm aware. Though apparently drunk Faye has a kink for wedding rings."

My eyes dropped to the evidence—a pair of matching wedding bands glinting on our fingers. Mine was a thinner, more delicate ring, a slim band with a twisted design, like two vines intertwined with tiny sapphires and diamonds. The metal shimmered faintly, catching the light in unexpected ways. It was beautiful and unconventional, but tough enough for a girl who spent most of her days on the road with a rock band.

Sam held up his hand, angling his ring under the light, a hint of a grin tugging at his lips His was a thick band of brushed silver, understated but rugged, with a subtle edge that suited him perfectly.

"Looks like you've got good taste, Mrs. Dogg," he teased, the title sending a tiny thrill down my spine.

I shoved the feeling aside, hiding my unease behind my glare. "Don't push it."

He returned to the article. "*Dogg said of Moyo in a recent interview with* Vanity Fair, '*Faye is the glue that keeps this band together. She's more than a publicist—though her marketing genius is unparalleled. She's as much a member of the band as I am.*'" He glanced up. "I stand by that."

"I know. Keep reading."

"It ends with, '*Perhaps this relationship isn't as surprising as we've been led to believe.*'"

He chuckled, far too relaxed for the media

nightmare we'd drunkenly catapulted ourselves into.

"Is this a laughing matter?" I asked, fidgeting with the bedsheets as my mind raced with ways to minimize the damage. "We're going to have to organize an annulment. That won't be hard considering we didn't consummate the marriage. Wait." I sat up. "We didn't consummate, right?"

Sam gestured at my dress. "No."

I breathed a sigh of relief and sank back against the bed. "Then we should definitely contact the lawyers. Do you think—"

"Hey," he interrupted, placing a hand on my shoulder. "Breathe."

During most PR crises, I could be counted upon to be an oasis of calm. An island of competence and serenity in a sea of chaos. I'd steered us through crazed fans, false tax evasion allegations, dating and relationship disasters, and more than one media misstep with poise and grace.

In the face of my own crisis, it appeared that all sense of calm had vanished, leaving behind a growing avalanche of panic.

"Breathe?" I repeated, swinging my arms out wildly. "What do you mean, breathe? We're fucked six ways to Friday, Sam. My professional reputation is in tatters. Our work relationship is *destroyed.* I can never show my face in the Cove again!"

As I tumbled into an emotional black hole, Sam seemed determined to save me from despair.

"It's not that bad."

I jabbed a finger at his phone. "We're on the front freaking page of the *Chars Times*, Samuel! Are you going to tell me that's not about to be picked up by—Gods forbid—the goddamned international press?"

He shrugged. "It's a slow news day. Something new will pop up."

I fumbled with my bra, tugging out my cell to shove at him. "I have two hundred and forty-three missed calls and over a thousand text messages!"

"Sounds like an average day for you."

"Men!"

Sam grinned at me—the same grin that sent millions of hearts a flutter every time he performed on stage.

"Oh no." I waggled my finger at him in warning. "You can't charm your way out this one, buddy."

"Honestly, Faye. I don't see what the big deal is. If anything, this is a boost to our ratings before the tour kicks off next week."

I pinched the bridge of my nose with my

free hand, desperately trying to ignore the pounding in my head. "I hate you."

"Shh, that's just the pain talking."

"Yeah, the pain in my ass," I muttered, shooting him a glare that told him exactly what, or in this case *who*, was the source of the pain.

He grinned and ducked his head to scroll on his phone. "You know, being married isn't a bad thing."

"No? Enlighten me."

"There's an article here called, 'Five Ways Being Married Is Good For You.'"

"Does it include murdering your spouse and inheriting their millions?" I asked sweetly.

"It includes personal growth, health, longevity, life satisfaction, and happiness."

"All of which I can achieve as a single woman who loves herself."

Sam cocked an eyebrow. "What about orgasms?"

"I believe a vibrator and my hand can take care of that."

He leaned back in his chair, slipping his cell into his pocket. "Romance is wasted on you."

"And the gravity of this situation is wasted on *you*."

My phone buzzed, and I hauled it out of my bra to see my best friend's smiling face lighting up the screen.

"Don't freak out," I said by way of greeting.

"Too late." Hope's warm drawl practically dripped with amusement. "Your brother already text me—not that I needed the update, you're all over the news. Married, Faye? To Sam? Really?"

I groaned. "I know, this is a disaster."

"Is it? Because from where I'm sitting in Grandma's kitchen, it looks like you finally let yourself have something you wanted instead of something you planned."

I winced at the reminder. We normally spent New Year's together, dancing off into the night. But her grandmother had experienced some health issues over the last year and Hope had agreed to move back to Peach Springs, a small town in Georgia, to care for her.

I missed Hope like crazy and despised that we didn't get to hang out much anymore.

"That's exactly the problem! I don't do unplanned, Hope. I don't do spontaneous. I definitely don't do drunken Vegas-style weddings with my client!"

"First, it wasn't Vegas. Second, Sam's more than your client and we both know it."

More than my client? He was my friend, sure. A good friend. A great friend, even. But it was ridiculous of her to suggest he might be anything more. Absolutely positively ridiculous. He and I made no sense.

And yet...

I sank onto the bed, cutting him a look.

He raised his eyebrows, taking the hint. "I'll just go get some coffee."

I watched him leave, for some reason finding my gaze stuck to his ass.

Stupid concussion.

"Okay, I can speak. He's stepped out."

Hope chuckled. "See? He's a good guy. You could have done worse."

"He's my friend."

"Mmhmm. And how many 'friends' do you bake birthday cupcakes for at 3am because they mentioned once that a foster mom used to make them?"

My cheeks heated, memories of that night flooding back—me in my kitchen at an ungodly hour, exhausted but carefully measuring out ingredients because Sam had casually mentioned something nostalgic over lunch.

"That was... professional courtesy."

"Sure it was, sugar. Just like those late-night phone calls about his songwriting are 'professional development.'"

"Hope—" I didn't have the capacity to consider this right now.

"I'm just saying, maybe this isn't the disaster

you think it is. Maybe it's the universe giving you a chance to explore something new."

"The universe should mind its own business."

Her laugh was warm and familiar. "Love is the universe's business."

"Says the romance novelist."

She snorted. "Don't try to change the subject. Tell me everything. And I mean *everything*."

I winced, feeling exposed, like she'd peeled back a layer I wasn't ready for her to see. There was too much swirling inside me—confusion, embarrassment, a nagging ache that maybe, just maybe, she'd hit on something real, something I wasn't ready to admit even to myself.

I closed my eyes against the bright lights of the room. "Do you mind if I call you tomorrow instead? I think I might have a concussion."

"Shit, how?"

I cleared my throat, mumbling into the phone.

"Did you say you fainted and are at the hospital?"

I made a noise of affirmation.

"Damn, girl, what a wild wedding night. Go rest. Text when you feel better."

"I will. Love you."

"Love you too, Faye. Be safe. And remember —Sam is one of the good ones."

Sam *was* one of the good ones. The kind of good that felt rare, almost too rare to belong to someone like me. And maybe that was what terrified me most—the idea that I'd fallen for someone without even realizing it, that this chaotic, spontaneous mess of a night was more than just a mistake.

Nope. Not going there. This is a mistake fuelled by booze and good cheer. Nothing more, nothing less.

It had to be. Anything else would be unacceptable.

I slipped my phone back into my bra, only to for it to buzz once again as Sam returned to the room.

I pulled out the offending object as he retook his seat, tossing it on the bed. "Deal with that, would you?"

"Isn't that your job?" he asked, picking up my phone.

"I'm taking a personal day." I forced myself to relax against the thin, plastic mattress, closing my eyes to the brightness of the room.

"Hello?" Sam answered the phone. "Ah, Mr. Moyo, lovely to speak to you."

I jerked upright, reaching across the bed to

grab the phone from Sam. The bastard stood, walking away from me.

"Give it to me," I hissed, my heart slamming against my chest as Sam ignored me.

"Yes, sir. We're at the hospital. Faye's had a bit of a fall and appears to be concussed." Sam nodded as he listened to whatever my dad was saying on the other end of the line. "I understand, sir. If you like, I can arrange to fly you out here today if that might give you and Mrs. Moyo some comfort?"

I shook my head frantically and immediately regretted the movement as a tidal wave of nausea burned up my throat. I grabbed frantically for the collapsible vomit bag beside the bed. I heard a clatter, then Sam was there, sweeping up my braids and holding them back as I vomited into the plastic bag.

"Oh gods," I groaned as my world spun wildly. "I'm going to kill whoever thought footboards made of wood were a good idea."

Sam gently took the bag away, disposing of it as I lay back, pressing the icepack to my aching forehead.

"Close your eyes," he said, gently holding a small cup of water to my lips. "Rest while I finish talking to your parents."

I took the cup, swishing water around my

mouth as I listened, too dizzy, in pain, and embarrassed to stop him.

"Sorry for dropping the phone. Faye needed my help." Sam plucked the cup from my hands, placing it on the bedside table. "I understand. It's been a surprise for us too."

I closed my eyes, desperate to silence the pounding in my head.

"Yes, sir. Sorry, yes, Chidi."

That was enough to have me opening my eyes. My father had *not* permitted any of my previous boyfriends to call him by his first name.

"I will. I'll call you as soon as I know more. Yes, sir—I mean, Chidi. Bye."

I watched Sam through narrowed eyes as he turned back to me, balking at my look.

"What?" he asked defensively.

"Are you on a first name basis with my father?"

Sam ignored the question. "How are you feeling?"

"Like Wile E. Coyote is blowing up dynamite in my brain."

"Wow, way to age yourself."

I snorted. "Sorry, should I have said Perry the Platypus? And don't think I don't see you deflecting. Answer the question."

Sam frowned. "Should we call a nurse?

Want me to see if we can get you some pain relief?"

"No, I want to know about you and my dad."

Sam cleared his throat, a slight blush creeping up his neck.

"Samuel," I growled in warning.

"We're in the same fantasy football league. We text regularly."

I blinked, then blinked again. "Did you say you *text* with my father? The man who hates texting and would rather crawl across the continent than type out so much as a single letter?"

"Maybe he hates texting with you, but the guy blows up my DMs." Sam handed me his phone. "Look."

I scrolled slowly, unable to comprehend the volume of trash talk—including emojis and gifs—my father and Sam exchanged.

"Dear Lord," I whispered, handing the phone back to Sam. "You're dating my dad. My entire life is a lie."

My bombshell realization was interrupted by a cheerful nurse holding a small paper cup.

"Good news," she said, shaking the cup gently. "The doctor has approved some painkillers while you wait for the results. These'll help take the edge off. Though, be warned, they might make you a little loopy or sleepy."

I didn't give a shit so long as they helped with the pain.

I downed the pills, chasing them with a shot of water, while she checked my vitals.

"Any other changes apart from the vomiting and dizziness?"

"No."

"Good." She made a note on my file, then tucked it into the board at the bottom of the bed. "Alright, shouldn't be much longer. We're just waiting for a final check of the CT, then the doctor will be back to explain the results to you. Just hit that buzzer if you need anything."

The pills took over quickly, easing the pain and leaving me with a euphoric, floating feeling.

"I wonder if this is what flying feels like," I muttered, enjoying the sensation. "Do you think if we inhaled enough helium we could fly?"

Sam snorted. "I doubt it. I think you'd end up suffocating way before that."

I raised both arms gently undulating them. "We should fly away. That'd quiet the press."

"We're not flying away."

I dropped my arms. "Then we should stay married."

Sam brushed a hand across my arm. "What?"

I peeked at him from under the icepack. "We should stay married. Until the end of the tour. It'll generate interest from your fans, and intrigue from the press. Then it'll all settle down and we can quietly annul after the tour when we're not constantly in front of the media."

Sam frowned. "You'd be willing to do that?"

"Sure." I closed my eyes again. "But only if you give me a raise. And a prenup. Don't want you stealing all my debt."

He snorted, sweeping a loose braid back as he gently stroked my cheek. "Sleep, Faye. I'll work something out."

"Okay," I agreed, and promptly did just that.

3

SAM

- The Wild Ones, "Stage Manager"

~

Faye glared at me from across the tour bus.

She'd been doing that a lot since we'd woken up with rings on our fingers and a marriage license on the bedside table.

Fuck. That'd been a shock. Waking up in Faye's bed with her looking like fucking smoke show even after a full night of drinking and drama with smudged makeup and a crumpled dress? Damn. Happy New Year's to me.

Her immediately fainting and knocking her head on the side of the bed? Not so great.

The memories of last night were hazy, like the edges of an old photograph, but I'd managed to recall a few details—her laughing as we danced, the flash of a neon-lit chapel, my own voice slurring out a "Fuck yes!" as someone slipped a ring into my hand.

I glanced down at the band on my finger, feeling the cool, solid weight of the metal. A sharp ache had taken up residence in my chest, a reckless kind of satisfaction that felt both irrational and persistent.

I glanced back up to find Faye still glaring at me, her eyes narrowed as she told me silently that she didn't find our situation funny at all.

"Don't give me that look," I told her, unreasonably amused by her reaction. "You've done this to us more times than I can count."

She crossed her arms across her chest, arching a delicate eyebrow. "This is my job."

"Not today," her assistant, Liz, said cheerfully. "Today *you're* the story."

I ignored the snickers from my fellow bandmates as Faye's cheeks took on a dark flush.

Joining us were Justice, Felix, and Radley—my fellow Wild Ones. Not too long ago, we were a pack of ramshackle kids who happened to strike it big. Now, we were about to undertake the next leg of our world tour.

Our appearances certainly reflected the change in our circumstances. Where before we were all rough edges and cheap clothes; now, we were primped and prodded, dressed in designer gear from the top of our heads to the tips of our toes.

"Have to say I'm enjoying sitting on this side of the table," Justice drawled from where he lay sprawled across his bunk in the bus—a guitar in one hand as he absently plucked at strings. Tattoos decorated each arm and peeked out the top of his V-neck shirt. A shirt for which I'd given him shit more than once. Though our lead singer didn't care, he'd simply smoothed a hand over his dark hair, and grinned at me, throwing his arms out as he'd proclaimed he was giving the fans exactly what they wanted.

Based on the explicit fan emails I happened to read occasionally, he wasn't wrong.

"How are you not hung over?" I asked him, tossing a guitar pick at his head.

He ignored it, strumming slowly. "When one doesn't drink, one doesn't get drunk."

Radley ignored him. "It's certainly a treat to see Faye on the receiving end of one of these," she said, tossing her curly brown hair. "And Sam as well? Christmas has come late—or is it early?—this year."

I made an "aw shucks" gesture.

"Should we be documenting this?" Felix asked, grinning widely when Faye turned her glare on him.

"Hush," Liz admonished, finally getting her iPad to connect with the TV screen hanging from the roof of the bus. "What does Faye always say in these moments?"

"We're here to help, not judge," we recited in unison.

"Gonna admit, you should all call me Judge Judy 'cause I certainly am." Felix held up two fingers about an inch apart. "But only a little."

"You are all terrible and I hate you," Faye sniffed.

"Children, quiet! It's my time to shine." Liz hit the screen of the iPad, then cursed under her breath when the TV didn't do anything.

"For goodness sake, sis. Let me." Felix reached across the table to pluck the iPad from his sister's hand. The twins shared the same dark-red hair, freckled skin, and big bellowing laugh.

"Thank you," she said primly when he got the slide deck to appear on the screen. "Let's begin, shall we?"

I crossed my ankles and leaned back in my seat, already amused by the whole situation.

Who would have thought one little marriage would cause so many issues?

"In the last eight hours, you've been trending across most major news outlets—and that includes internationally." Liz clicked to her first slide—a sample of the different media stories.

"The good news is, most of the articles are positive and generating sales for the tour." She clicked to the next slide, showing the increase in sales.

"I feel a 'but' coming," I said.

"But," Liz echoed. "Some sites are spreading salacious rumors in what appears to be a clickbait effort."

She moved to the next slide, and I winced. The headlines implied Faye had been injured in a fight with me. No surprises given her injury, but damn if it didn't hurt to see them accusing me of hurting Faye—one of the most important people in my life.

They could smear my name as a dick or a diva or a drunk all they wanted, but to accuse me of that? Fuck.

I glanced over at Faye in time to catch her touching the thick plaster they'd applied to her forehead. Seeing that turned the possessive, protective ache in my chest into a full-blown blaze. And there was nothing I could do to alleviate the throb.

She'd been released an hour ago—under strict instructions she not be alone and to return if her symptoms worsen—and security had hustled us out of the hospital and onto the bus, as we had to head to our next gig—shitty timing, I know.

I didn't mind the bus life—despite the lack of privacy. It gave us all a chance to collaborate and connect without cameras or fans. Or potential stalkers. I'd once come back from a gig to find a hotel concierge sniffing my underwear. Not cool.

The tour bus was a beast of a double-decker, painted jet black with The Wild Ones logo emblazoned on the side in silver and electric blue. The bus looked like it had seen its fair share of highways, with a few subtle dings here and there that only added to its gritty charm. It was a rolling fortress—a mix of comfort and chaos—tailored for the long, unpredictable months on the road with a rock band.

Inside, the lower deck opened into a small but surprisingly cozy lounge area. Worn leather couches lined the walls, creating a semicircle around a low table, which was currently littered with crumpled setlists, half-empty coffee cups, and a pair of drumsticks that one of the roadies had forgotten to pack. Across from the lounge was a compact kitchen, equipped with a mini-fridge crammed with soda, a microwave, and a coffee maker that looked like it had survived a war. The walls were decorated with posters from past tours and taped-up Polaroids of the band and crew, each capturing memories from life on the road.

Up a narrow staircase, the sleeping quarters took up the entire second deck. Ten bunks were lined up in tight rows along the walls, each with a curtain for privacy. The bunks were compact but surprisingly comfortable, with just enough room for a person to stretch out, stash a phone and book, and plug in a set of noise-cancelling headphones. The ceiling was low, giving the whole space an intimate, almost cocooned feel. At the very back was a small but functional bathroom—an undeniable luxury in our world of endless highways and dive bars.

I would have preferred Faye to be upstairs resting than working.

"You sure you're okay to be discussing this nonsense?" I asked Faye.

She nodded, brushing aside my concerns. "We need to get ahead of the story. We're already hours behind. If we leave it much longer, we lose the narrative."

I gestured at the table. "We can handle it. You should rest. Take some more of those pain pills."

Faye shot me an annoyed look. "I'm *fine*. Now, can we please get on with the briefing?"

I bit my tongue to keep from pressing her further, gesturing at Liz to continue.

"It took me a few minutes to work out where the leak came from, but let's just say you guys weren't exactly subtle when it came to hitching your wagons."

She clicked to the next slide, and I winced as the rest of the table burst out laughing.

"Oh, good Lord," Faye muttered, covering her face with a hand.

We'd been married by a guy in a unicorn suit.

"It seems," Liz said, her tone dripping with amusement, "the Little Chapel in Chars is famous for their eccentric celebrant options.

And apparently you two decided on an Urma the Unicorn rip-off."

The adult cartoon we were all obsessed with. It had started as a sarcastic comic strip a few years ago, before moving to become a webcomic, then a fully animated streaming show.

"Definitely off-brand," I agreed, touching the ring nestled on my third finger of my left hand. I hadn't ever been one to wear jewelry, but the weight of it felt good, heavy, solid.

Real.

Unfortunately, the unicorn wedding photo wasn't the worst of it.

"Please tell me there isn't more," Faye groaned as Liz just clicked to the next slide with barely contained glee.

There we were, standing outside the chapel, my arm around Faye's waist as she brandished a bouquet made entirely of drumsticks.

"I have to admit," Radley said, leaning forward to study the image. "That's actually kind of genius."

"The fans are going crazy over it," Felix added, scrolling through his phone. "Someone's already started an Etsy shop selling rip-off bouquets."

I couldn't take my eyes off Faye in the photo. Even with her sophisticated red dress wrinkled from hours of celebration and her braids slightly mussed but still elegant, she looked radiant. She wasn't just beautiful; she was breathtaking. The kind of breathtaking that hits you right in the chest, leaving you stunned and slightly off-balance.

I swallowed, forcing myself to don the same mask I'd work every day for the last five years. I had to pretend this didn't get to me. That *she* didn't get to me.

But hell, how could I *not* notice her?

The high-definition photo had captured in loving detail every part of her that drove me insane—the smooth lines of her collarbone, the way that dress hugged her curves, her full lips curved in a smile that I wanted to think was just for me, even though I knew better. I'd seen the smile that lit up her face only a few times—at her brother's wedding, at our signing with the label, and now at our sham of a wedding.

She reminded me of a butterfly—always moving. You got a sense of beauty from watching her, but it wasn't until she paused long enough to let you near that you understood just how breathtaking she was.

She always had been. Always would be.

I'd gotten used to admiring her from a distance, trying not to notice the way her brown eyes sparkled when she teased, or the curve of her lips when she smiled, or the soft slope of her neck that I'd found my gaze lingering on too many times to count.

My gaze dropped to where our hands were linked in the photo, and I could practically feel her warmth, a ghost of the way her body had leaned against me, as if, for just that one moment, she was mine.

You're friends, I reminded myself for the billionth time. *Just friends.*

But putting her back into that box when a ring sat snug against my finger felt almost sacrilegious.

But I'd do it. Because Faye meant more to me than a quick lay or some foolish kiss. She deserved more.

"Moving on," Liz said, interrupting my thoughts. "We need to establish our story and stick to it."

"The truth?" I suggested, earning a collective groan from the band.

"The truth being that you both got wasted and decided getting married by a guy in a unicorn costume was a good idea?" Justice asked, still plucking at his guitar. "Yeah, that'll play great with the press."

"Actually..." Faye straightened in her seat, her PR brain clearly kicking into gear despite the concussion. "Think about it. What's the one criticism we always get? That we're too polished, too manufactured. This"—she gestured between us—"this is real. Messy. Human."

I watched her as she spoke, remembering our conversation in the hospital. The way she'd suggested we stay married until the end of the tour.

I'd thought it was just the drugs talking, but now...

"She's right," Radley chimed in. "Our fans would eat it up. The ultra-professional PR manager and the laid-back guitarist, falling in love right under everyone's noses? A secret romance is just the thing we need right now."

"And the timeline works," Felix pointed out. "You've been with us for five years. Friends-to-lovers will play well. Forced proximity, maybe one bed in the bus." He wiggled his bushy eyebrows suggestively.

The bus hit a bump, and Faye winced, touching her bandaged forehead. I reached for her automatically, steadying her with a hand on her shoulder.

"You okay?"

She nodded, but I could see the pain in her eyes.

"Just need a minute." She sucked in a deep breath. "Okay, here's what we're going to do. Liz, pull up any pictures of Sam and I from the last five years that you can find. Post them on socials with a quip like, 'Ringing in the new year' or some such shit. Include the wedding picture but get permission from the OG poster, first. Check if the chapel has any pictures as well, and go through our phones to see what else Sam and I might have recorded in our drunken state." She barely paused for breath.

"I want you to tee up a few choice quotes from the band about our close friendship. See if any of our family or friends—hell, even the label—are willing to congratulate us. Put out a press release saying how pleased we all are about the marriage, but frame it to focus on the next leg of the tour and note we'll honeymoon later. We want to make it clear to the fans they come first. Hit up one of our trusted journalists and agree to an exclusive in a few days—a week, if possible. That'll give us time to work out our stories, and for my head to heal. Address the rumor about my hospital stay directly—release the medical info, if required."

I frowned. "You're really going to allow them to print that you hurt your head on the edge of our bed?"

Faye shot me a look. "We'll get Justice to gently fuel rumors that you're a sex god and it occurred mid-coitus. So shut it."

I zipped my lips, grinning.

"I'm not sure I consent to being used like this," Justice said lightly.

Faye ignored him. "Next, I want you to—"

The bus hit another bump, and Faye's face drained of color. She pressed a hand to her mouth, closing her eyes.

"That's enough for today," I announced, standing abruptly. "We can figure out the rest later."

"But—" Faye began.

"Nope. Doctor's orders were rest." I offered her my hand. "Come on. Liz can take care of the rest of this shit. Trust us, we've got this. It's time for you to get some sleep."

She narrowed her eyes but took my hand. Quietly alarmed by her easy acquiesce, I helped her to her feet, pretending not to notice when she swayed slightly, leaning against me.

"We're not done discussing this," she warned as I guided her up the stairs and toward the back of the bus where the private bunks were located.

"Never thought we were," I replied, helping her climb into her bunk. I reached for her overnight bag, pulling out her silk bonnet—the dark purple one with little silver stars that Radley had gifted her for her birthday last year.

"Here," I said, handing it to her. "Can't have

you waking up with your edges all messed up. Your mama would kill me."

That got a small laugh out of her. "Look at you, being all educated."

"I pay attention." I shrugged, watching as she carefully wrapped her braids. "Plus, your mom gave me a whole lecture about it when we were home last summer."

"That sounds like her," Faye said softly, settling back against her pillows, already looking drowsy. "Sam?"

"Mm?"

"What if this ruins everything?"

I caught her hand before she could pull it away, giving her a gentle squeeze.

"Hey, look at me." I waited until she met my gaze, struck as always by how her eyes seemed to hold flecks of gold in certain lights. "Nothing's ruined. We're still us. Still The Wild Ones. Today you're a little battered and bruised, but tomorrow you'll be fighting fit, keeping us all in check while we drive you crazy."

A small smile tugged at her lips. "You are pretty good at that last part."

"It's a gift." I grinned, then grew serious. "Get some rest, Faye. We'll figure it out tomorrow." I kissed her nose and turned to leave.

Her voice stopped me. "Sam?"

"Yeah?"

"Thanks for not freaking out."

I looked back at her. She seemed so little and unsure in her bed, vulnerable thanks to the plaster peeking out from under her bonnet.

Something shifted in my chest, the ring on my left hand feeling a fraction lighter. "Don't worry, Faye. We'll come out of this stronger."

With a small sigh, her eyelashes fluttered, and she closed her eyes. "We'll see."

Yeah. We would.

4

FAYE

MORNING ASSESSMENT & COMPATIBILITY REVIEW

Priority Level: HIGH
Status: UNEXPECTEDLY INTIMATE

IMMEDIATE OBSERVATIONS:
☐ Sam makes perfect coffee
☐ Knows my breakfast preferences
☐ Wearing my favorite hoodie
☐ Domesticity level: Dangerous
☐ Heart: Malfunctioning

THINGS TO DISCUSS:
1. Wedding night details
2. Boundaries during tour
3. PR strategy

4. Why my stomach flips when he
smiles
Note: STRIKE LAST ITEM
IMMEDIATELY

CURRENT CONCERNS:
A) How good Sam looks in the
morning
B) Personal/Professional lines
blurring
Note: Focus on professional
aspects ONLY

Threat Level: INCREASING
Personal Note: Stop noticing his
dimples
Secondary Note: Stop making notes
about Sam
Final Note: This is getting out
of hand

~

Despite the concussion, my internal body clock woke me up at 5am. The bus hummed quietly beneath us as we rolled through the pre-dawn darkness, and for a moment, I forgot about marriages and media storms lying there, listening to the soft snores and sniffles of the sleeping people around me.

At least I did until I touched the bandage on my head.

Time to get to work.

Sliding from my bunk, I opened the small cupboard beside it, quietly pulling out some clothes before making my way to the full bathroom at the rear of the bus.

Dressed, I made my way downstairs and found Sam in the small kitchen area, his back to me as he worked the coffee maker with practiced movements. He wore low-slung sweatpants and a soft gray t-shirt that had seen better days, his dark hair still messy from sleep.

"Extra hot, triple shot," he said without turning. "Give me two minutes."

"How did you know it was me?"

He glanced over his shoulder, a soft smile playing at his lips. "You're the only one who gets up this early. Plus"—his eyes tracked down my body—"I recognized the shuffle of those ridiculous unicorn slippers."

"Hey, don't mock Mr. Sparkles and Sir Glitter." I hoisted myself onto the counter, watching as he moved around the tiny kitchen with familiar ease. "They're very dignified."

"Keep telling yourself that, wife."

The title sent a shiver down my spine that I

chose to blame on the early morning chill. "About that..."

"Breakfast first." He placed a steaming mug in my hands – the oversized one with music notes that had somehow become "mine" over the years. "You're always grumpy before coffee."

"I am not—" I caught his knowing look and took a sip instead. Perfect, as always. "Fine. Feed me."

His laugh was quiet in deference to our sleeping bandmates. "The usual?"

"Please."

He pulled eggs and a loaf of bread from the mini-fridge and began to crack eggs into a pan with practiced ease.

"Did you sleep well?"

I raised one shoulder in a half shrug. "It was fine."

He cocked an eyebrow in question.

"The bus movement was a little much," I admitted. "Sometimes it was okay, sometimes I rolled and felt a little nauseous."

"I'll make sure we stop for tonight and the guys lock the bus down extra tight. Unless you want a hotel?"

"No, don't I'll be fine."

"Faye." He stopped whisking the eggs to glare at me. "Let me do this."

I hid a smile behind my mug. "Fine. But I

don't need a hotel. The extra straps on the bus will be fine."

Sam poured my eggs into the pan, spinning it until the mess covered the bottom. "Is that why you're stressed?"

"I'm not stressed."

"No? Then why are you stealing my hoodie?"

I glanced down at the worn fabric drowning my frame—definitely his. I hated that he knew one of my stress tells. "This isn't yours."

"It has my name on the back."

I kicked him with one of my slippers. "Shut up and cook my eggs."

His shoulders shook with silent laughter as he worked. I sipped my coffee, watching the way his muscles moved under his shirt, how his hands stayed steady even as the bus swayed beneath us.

"So," he said after a moment. "Should we talk about it?"

I breathed out a sigh. "The wedding or the aftermath?"

"Both?" He slid a perfect omelette onto a plate, adding a touch of salt and cracked pepper. He handed it to me, then leaned one hip against the counter as he crossed his arms, looking far too comfortable. "For two people who supposedly got married, we haven't really talked about the actual event. Only what came after."

"Well, it wasn't exactly *planned*," I replied, breaking off a piece of the omelette with my fork. "One minute, I was dancing. The next, I'm standing at an altar holding your hand while some Urma the Unicorn impersonator is trying not to laugh."

He chuckled, turning back to the bench as the toaster popped with his toast. "I think it was your idea."

I blinked. "Are you serious?"

He pulled his phone from his pocket, tossing it to me. "Look."

Sure enough, there I was on his lock screen, crouched in the snow as I proposed to him.

"Tequila and I do not mix," I muttered, shaking my head. "I must have lost my goddamned mind."

We were quiet for a minute as I watched him bustle about the kitchen.

"You didn't have to go through with it, you know." I looked up at him, meeting his gaze. "So why did you?"

He paused as he buttered his toast, his expression thoughtful. "Honestly? I don't know. Maybe I just didn't want to see you walk away."

The words hung between us, warm and unexpected. I wasn't ready to unpack that, wasn't ready to examine exactly what that meant.

He turned back to his toast, resuming spreading the butter. "Or maybe I just wanted the right to steal your clothes as well." He looked pointedly at his hoodie. "Do you think that red dress would match my coloring?"

I rolled my eyes. "You're an idiot."

"You love it," he murmured, picking up his plate and moving back to lean against the counter.

We ate side by side in silence, watching each other with gazes that lingered, as if we'd somehow crossed into new territory without realizing it.

"I have an idea," he said after swallowing. "Twenty questions. Anything we want to know about the wedding night or each other. Complete honesty."

"That sounds..."

"Terrifying?"

"I was going to say efficient." I forked another piece of egg. "You go first."

He grinned. "I'll start easy. What's my coffee order?"

"Well, firstly, you don't drink coffee. You're a black tea, two sugars before noon, or a black tea with honey after shows because your throat gets scratchy. Though you also secretly love those caramel milkshake monstrosities Justice gets but won't admit it because you think it ruins your image."

His eyebrows rose. "I'm unsurprised but still impressed. And I only like those caramel things 'cause of the cream. The actual drink is trash."

I stabbed my fork in his direction. "My turn. What do you remember about the wedding?"

"Snippets. The unicorn guy. You laughing at his jokes. Dancing to 'Brown Eyed Girl' in the parking lot." His smile turned thoughtful. "You looked happy."

"I was drunk."

"Yeah, we both were." Something flickered in his expression. "But it was nice, seeing you let go for once."

I ducked my head. "Your turn."

"Why haven't you dated since Alex?"

Oof.

I sucked in a breath, focusing on my plate to buy time. "I've been busy."

"Hmmm."

"What?" I looked up at him. "What's with the 'hmmm'?"

He tilted his head, studying me. "I don't know. Feels like there's more to it than that."

I shrugged, deflecting. "Alright, my question. Was I really the one who suggested the wedding?"

He laughed, tipping his head back. "Oh, absolutely. You leaned over, grabbed my hand, and said something about 'making memories' or maybe it was 'making a mess.' Hard to tell with all the tequila."

I groaned. "Fantastic. Remind me to stay far, far away from spirits."

"My turn." He tapped a finger against his lip. "Okay, what's my best quality?"

I pretended to think it over, spearing the final bite of my omelette. "Definitely your ability to fix breakfast."

He snorted. "Glad I'm useful."

"But," I added, jabbing him with a toe. "You're loyal. Fiercely loyal. Once you care about someone, you're all in."

He looked away for a second, a rare flicker of uncertainty crossing his face. "Your turn."

"Kids? See them in your future?"

He shrugged. "I'm undecided which I guess is a no. I'm of the opinion that unless you're a hundred percent in, then you shouldn't be bringing kids into the world."

I winced. "I didn't think before asking that question. Sorry."

"Don't be. I know what it's like to grow up with a parent who didn't want you—just thought they might once upon a time. And I know what it's like to grow up with a parent who actually wants you."

"Will," I said, referring to Sam's adopted dad.

"Yeah." He reached behind him, lifting the coffee pot to top me up. "He's a good guy. Having him for a dad cemented it for me. I won't bring kids into the world unless I have zero doubts. The fact I'm undecided means I'm a no. And I don't see that changing any time soon."

I hesitated. "I don't want kids. I mean, I love being Auntie Faye and will always be on call, but when I think about my life, I don't envision kids for me."

"What about a partner?"

I placed my empty plate to the side, wrapping my hands around my coffee mug and taking a sip before answering. "I hope so but I'm also happy alone. Another person needs to enhance my life, not improve it."

"Oof, deep thoughts for this early in the morning." Sam placed his mug in the sink. "Last question."

I hesitated. "What do you think will happen after the tour? With... us?"

He was quiet for a long time, his gaze fixed somewhere past my shoulder. Finally, he straightened, placing one hand on either side of the bench as he leaned into me.

Our gazes locked as he leaned in.

"After the tour, I hope we'll—"

"Sam! Faye!" Justice's voice boomed from upstairs. "Emergency band meeting!"

I startled, nearly spilling my coffee. Sam caught it smoothly, his hands encompassing mine around the mug.

"Saved by the bellowing idiot," he murmured.

"Sam—" I wanted to break the tension, but the words died as his fingers lingered on mine, warm and steady. His touch held a quiet promise, as if he could feel the unsteady beat of tension humming under my skin.

"We're not done with this conversation." He squeezed my hands. "But this is a conversation for when we're alone." His thumb brushed over my knuckles, soft, teasing, gentle, before he gently tugged the cup from my hand.

As I watched him head upstairs, carrying my coffee as if he hadn't just scrambled my emotions. I wrapped my arms around my middle, willing myself to push him back into the box in which he'd dwelled. Friends. We were friends.

But his parting words left me to wonder exactly what he hoped we might be.

5

FAYE

INTERVIEW PROTOCOL

Priority Level: CRITICAL
Status: BARELY HOLDING IT TOGETHER

PRESENTATION REQUIREMENTS:
☐ Project happy newlyweds
☐ Maintain professional boundaries
☐ Stop rewriting this list
(attempt #7)
☐ Breathe normally when Sam's
nearby
☐ Remember rehearsed responses

KEY TALKING POINTS:
1. Natural progression of
friendship

2. Perfect timing with tour
3. Private ceremony (DO NOT
MENTION UNICORN)
4. Mutual respect and admiration
5. NO MENTION OF TEQUILA

CONTINGENCY PLANS:
A) Deflect personal questions
B) Redirect to tour discussion
C) Emergency exit strategy
D) Resist urge to sniff Sam
Note: WHAT IS THIS COLOGNE???

REMEMBER:
- This is just another interview
- Everything is under control
- Sam's thumb stroking my shoulder
means nothing
- Stop adding notes about Sam

Current Status: T-minus 60 minutes
to interview
Threat Level: Escalating

Personal Note: This would be
easier if he'd stop looking at me
like that

Secondary Note: Stop making notes
about how he looks at me

Final Note: I am a PROFESSIONAL.
This is FINE.

~

"You're doing it again," Sam murmured, sliding a fresh cup of coffee across the small table in our shared tour bus kitchenette.

I didn't look up from my laptop where I was crafting our first official interview responses. "Doing what?"

"That thing where you forget to breathe when you're stressed."

I'd worked with Sam for five years. I'd seen how he anticipated the band's needs before they voiced them. How he noticed when Justice's voice strained or when Radley's wrists ached from too much drumming.

It shouldn't have surprised me how much he observed. And yet...

I glanced up to find him watching me with soft brown eyes. He wore a plain black t-shirt that hung loose on his frame, his dark hair still damp from his shower. The early morning light caught the wedding ring on his left hand as he lifted his own cup to his lips.

My heart did a strange little flip that I blamed entirely on a caffeine overdose despite having yet to take a sip of my second cup.

"I'm not stressed," I lied. "I'm energized."

His lips twitched. "You've rewritten that email six times."

"You've been counting?"

He shrugged, taking another sip of his tea. "You pull your bottom lip between your teeth when you're overthinking, and your left eye twitches when you're lying."

I reached up to touch the corner of my eye, scowling when his grin widened.

"Made you look."

"Shouldn't you be warming up or something? The interview's in an hour."

The band were slated for a morning show interview and performance. Tomorrow night would be their first performance on this leg of the tour, and in the craziness of the last day, I'd completely blanked on this interview.

Thankfully, Liz had remembered and called a band meeting. We were due at the studio around eight for a nine o'clock performance, followed by a nine thirty interview. Which meant I had precisely twenty-one minutes before all hell was about to break loose.

"I'm good." He settled back in his chair, still watching me with that infuriating mix of amusement and concern. "Want to tell me what's bothering you?"

I gestured at my laptop. "Other than crafting responses to deeply personal questions about our relationship while trying to maintain professional boundaries and not tank both our careers?"

"Other than that."

A laugh escaped before I could catch it. That was the thing about Sam; he had a way of making even the most stressful situations seem manageable.

I closed my laptop, wrapping my hands around my coffee cup. "I don't want to mess this up for you. For the band."

"Hey." He reached across the table, his fingers brushing my wrist. "You've never messed up anything. You're the reason we've made it this far."

"That's not—"

"Remember that incident with Justice and the llama?"

I smiled. "That was different."

"Or the time Felix accidentally started that cult?"

"That wasn't actually a cult," I corrected automatically. "Just some very enthusiastic fans who misinterpreted his tweet about starting a cheese appreciation society."

"My point is"—Sam's thumb brushed over my pulse point—"you've handled everything we've thrown at you. This is just another day at the office."

"Except I'm usually handling other people's crises. Not starring in my own."

"True." He withdrew his hand, and I tried not to notice how I missed his warmth. "But now you've got me to help handle it."

Before I could respond, Justice's voice boomed from the back of the bus. "If you two lovebirds are done canoodling, we've got a show to prepare for."

I straightened in my chair, professionalism snapping back into place like armor. "No one says canoodling anymore."

"I do," Justice appeared in the kitchenette doorway, already dressed in his signature all-black ensemble. "And I'm a rockstar, so I make it cool."

"Keep telling yourself that," Sam murmured into his mug.

I stood, gathering my things. "The car will be here in forty-five minutes. Everyone remember their talking points?"

"Yes, dear," Sam drawled, earning him a glare.

"Don't call me dear."

"Sorry, sweetums."

"I will end you."

"Promises, promises, snookums."

Justice looked between us, shaking his head. "You know, for two people pretending to be married, you already bicker like an old couple."

I ignored the comment, just like I ignored the feeling of Sam's eyes following me as I left the kitchenette.

Just another day at the office.

Right.

~

THE SOUND STAGE lights burned hot against my skin as I watched from inside the studio as The Wild Ones performed "Wild Heart" out on the plaza stage. Like many morning shows, *Good Morning Today* had their own set up specifically for days like this.

And to land the band of the moment was quite the coup. Which meant they'd gone all out on the stage decorations for today.

"Two minutes!" the floor manager called out.

Liz appeared at my elbow, tablet in hand. "We've got this."

"Of course we do." I smoothed down my

pencil skirt, checking my reflection in my phone. The bandage on my forehead covered by a brightly patterned head wrap. "It's just another interview."

"Except this time you're the story."

I shot her a look. "Not helpful."

"Sorry." She didn't sound sorry at all. "But hey, at least Sam looks good."

I followed her gaze back to the TV screens. She wasn't wrong. The stylist had dressed him in dark jeans and a forest-green button-down that made his brown eyes appear almost golden under the lights. His hair had been artfully tousled, and his wedding ring caught the light every time he moved his hands.

They played one song then transitioned into another as Liz moved away, taking a call.

I nodded my head in time to the music, mentally running through the rest of our day.

"Faye?" Liz tapped me gently on my shoulder, pulling my attention from the screens. "There's someone here from the label."

I turned, my PR smile already in place, and felt it freeze on my face.

Alex Pontiff.

The sight of him hit me like ice water down my spine. He hadn't changed in the slightest since the last time I saw him, five years ago, when he'd ripped my world apart. If anything, he looked even more polished, every inch of him exuding that smug confidence I'd once found so intoxicating. His suit was immaculate —tailored to perfection in a deep navy that brought out the sharp lines of his jaw and his almost unsettlingly perfect cheekbones. His dark hair was swept back, not a strand out of place, adding to the impression of meticulous control that radiated from him like a force field. The faint scent of his expensive cologne drifted toward me, a crisp blend of something spicy and woodsy, as calculated as everything else about him.

But it was his eyes that really got me—still that same cool, calculating gray, sharp and assessing, with just a flicker of amusement beneath the surface. They'd once looked at me with warmth and admiration, or so I'd believed, but now I saw the truth. There was no warmth, only condescension hiding behind that well-practiced smile. His lips curved into a familiar, almost predatory grin that could easily pass as charming if you didn't know better.

"Hello, Faye."

His voice was exactly as I remembered it— smooth, with a hint of mockery wrapped in a thin layer of civility. He had the kind of tone that was impossible to pin down, teetering somewhere between polite professionalism and something far darker, like he was amused by the game he was playing and fully aware of the power he held.

"The label thought you might need some... assistance managing this situation," he said, letting the word "assistance" roll off his tongue with exaggerated patience, as though he was speaking to a child who'd once again gotten in over their head. The implication hung in the air, thick and suffocating: I'd messed up. Again. Just like last time.

My jaw clenched, but I forced myself to keep my expression neutral, even as every memory of that time came crashing back. The way he'd systematically sabotaged me, spread rumors about my so-called "unprofessionalism" and then swooped in to take credit for my work, leaving me with nothing but a shattered career and a bruised heart. He'd painted me as an unreliable mess, convincing the higher-ups I couldn't handle the pressure—all while wearing that exact same infuriatingly sympathetic smile.

"We have it handled," I said, proud of the steadiness in my voice despite the anger simmering beneath. "But thanks for your concern."

"Do you?" His eyebrow lifted as he glanced down at his phone, where no doubt the headlines were still blowing up with the band's impromptu wedding. "Because from where I'm standing, one of our biggest acts just had a drunken Vegas-style wedding that's trending across every social platform. Hardly seems... professional." The last word came out like a knife, aimed to wound, bringing with it all the old accusations he'd used to ruin me before.

I held his gaze, refusing to flinch, even as the memories clawed at the edges of my composure. *This time*, I told myself, *he won't get to see me crack.*

"First," I said, channeling every ounce of control I'd built since then, "it wasn't Vegas. Second, we've already implemented a comprehensive media strategy that's generating positive engagement and increased ticket sales for the tour."

"Ah yes, the 'secret romance' angle." His smile turned sharp. "Interesting choice. Almost makes one wonder if there were... previous entanglements. The kind that might constitute a conflict of interest."

The blood drained from my face as I caught his meaning. He was going to dig into my past with Sam, try to twist our connection into something inappropriate.

Just like he'd manipulated me into appearing "unreliable" five years ago.

"Is there a problem here?" Sam's arm settled around my back to rest on my hip, pulling me tight against his side.

I started, glancing up at him to find his jaw tight, his gaze trained on Alex.

I hadn't even noticed the band finishing their set.

"No problem," Alex said smoothly. "Just touching base about the situation. I'm Alex Pontiff, the label's new head of crisis management."

Sam's thumb grazed my hip absently, a subtle gesture of affection and comfort that made Alex's eyes narrow. "Funny, I don't remember the label mentioning they were sending anyone."

"It was a last-minute decision. Given the... delicate nature of the situation."

"The situation"—Sam's voice held an edge I rarely heard—"being what exactly?"

"A marriage that seems to have taken everyone by surprise." Alex's gaze slid to me. "Including, perhaps, the participants?"

Sam frowned. "What exactly are you saying?"

Alex lifted one shoulder in a half shrug. "I'm just suggesting that Faye isn't exactly known for her... reliability. It wouldn't be the first time that she made a mistake."

I would have stepped back had Sam's arm not tightened around me, holding me in place. My body reacted as if Alex words were a physical slap.

"You want to show some respect?" Sam snapped. "That's my wife you're speaking to."

My gaze flew to Sam, surprise warring with a delighted thrill at his possessive, defensive tone.

My wife.

"Thirty seconds!" the floor manager called out.

"You should take your place," I said, determined to shut down this conversation. "Liz, can you—?"

"Of course, I'll show Mr. Pontiff to the greenroom." Liz's gaze danced between us, quickly assessing the situation. I caught the concern in her eyes.

"Actually," Alex said, "I think I'll watch from here. Always good to observe how these situations... develop."

The implication was clear: he was watching me. Waiting for me to fail. Just like before.

Sam's hand dipped to press firmly against my back. "Faye?"

I looked up at him, finding warmth and worry in his dark eyes. He'd been there after Alex destroyed my career, had watched me rebuild myself piece by piece. He knew what this meant.

"I'm fine," I said, more for Alex's benefit than Sam's. "Go. You have a show to do."

Sam hesitated, then did something completely unexpected. He leaned down and kissed me—not the careful peck we'd planned for the cameras, but something softer, more intimate. He lingered.

"Love you," he murmured against my lips, loud enough for Alex to hear.

Then he was gone, joining the band on set as the lights came up.

I touched my lips, still feeling the phantom press of his kiss, trying to ignore the way Alex watched me with calculating eyes.

"Still mixing business with pleasure, I see," he said quietly.

I straightened my spine, channeling every ounce of control I'd built since he'd last torn me down. "The difference is, Alex, this time I know exactly who has my back."

"Do you?" His smile was sharp. "Because from where I'm standing, this looks an awful lot like history repeating itself."

"No," I said, watching as Sam settled onto the couch, his ring catching the studio lights. "This time I'm not the naive girl who trusted the wrong person. I'm the woman who rebuilt herself after you tried to destroy her."

"We'll see." He checked his watch. "The label wants a full report by end of day. Try not to... disappoint them."

The words hit their mark—he knew exactly how much that accusation would haunt me. I kept my face neutral as the cameras started rolling.

Sam glanced over, offering me a warm, encouraging smile.

But this time, I wasn't alone.

"I don't answer to you or the label," I informed Alex, drawing strength from Sam's quiet support. "I'm employed by the band. I'm their representative, not yours."

"Contracts are precarious things," he said in a soft voice. "Morality clauses and all that. You might want to ensure the band knows they're on the labels radar."

I gritted my teeth. "Noted."

The segment cut to a commercial break and one of the techs ran over. "Sam has requested you on set."

I blinked. "What?"

The tech began to mic me up, working quickly but efficiently. "He wants to introduce you."

"But—"

Alex stepped forward. "I think this is a bad idea. Perhaps we could—"

The tech ignored him, shoving me toward the set. "On the couch. We're back in forty-nine seconds."

I stumbled across the production floor toward where The Wild Ones sat arranged in a loose semicircle on the morning show's plush cream couches—Justice and Radley on one end, Felix in the middle, and Sam on the far right.

A spot had been conspicuously left open beside him, Amy Chen, the interviewer, hovering nearby.

I stepped onto the slightly raised set just as Amy's hand landed on Sam's shoulder.

Something hot and uncomfortable curled in my stomach.

Sam ignored her, standing up and crossing quickly to me.

"There you are." He held out his hand. "Was starting to think you'd changed your mind about being seen with us riffraff."

I took his hand, letting him guide me to the spot beside him. "Someone has to keep you lot in line."

His arm settled around my shoulders as I sat, the movement natural as breathing. "Always taking care of us."

"It's literally my job."

"Among other things now," Amy cut in with a bright smile that didn't quite reach her eyes. "Speaking of which, this surprise wedding has everyone talking! Tell us, how long have you two been secretly dating?"

"Ten seconds!" the floor manager called.

I opened my mouth to deliver our carefully rehearsed response, but Sam beat me to it.

"Actually," he said, his arm tightening slightly around my shoulders, "there's nothing secret about how much Faye means to the band. She's been our rock since day one."

"Five seconds!"

"But romantically—" Amy pressed.

"We're live in three, two..."

The red light blinked on, and Amy's picture-perfect smile snapped into place. "Welcome back to Good Morning Today, music lovers! I'm here with chart-topping sensation The Wild Ones, who are kicking off their world tour with some exciting news."

Sam's thumb brushed soothingly across my shoulder, and I realized I'd been holding my breath.

Just another interview, I reminded myself. Except this time, I couldn't hide in the wings.

"So"—Amy turned to us, her smile as polished as ever—"the whole world is dying to know, how does the band's publicist end up married to its lead guitarist?"

"Tequila," Justice deadpanned from the other end of the couch. "Lots and lots of tequila."

"What Justice means," I jumped in, my PR instincts taking over, "is that New Year's Eve was a celebration of many things. The end of a successful year, the start of our world tour, and yes, maybe we had a bit too much fun with the festivities." I could feel Sam's silent laughter beside me. "But Sam and I have known each other for years. And after being together for such a long time, the timing just felt right."

Amy's smile didn't waver, but there was a glint in her eye as she leaned forward, shifting to full-on interrogation mode, her voice syrupy sweet. "The timing is just so... interesting, don't you think?" she said, with a slight tilt of her head. "I mean, it's not every day that a band's publicist and its lead guitarist suddenly decide to get married. And right before a world tour launch, too! You can't blame people for wondering if there might have been a little... strategic planning involved?"

I kept my smile polite, feeling Sam tense beside me. "I understand how it might look that way," I replied, my PR instincts in full force, "but this wasn't about strategy. Like I said, we've known each other for years, and things just... fell into place."

She gave a small, skeptical nod, as though she was humoring me. "Of course, of course. But surely, as a publicist, you know the importance of timing. After all, you're not just any couple; you're both part of one of the biggest acts in the world right now. To the outside world, it looks like a bit of a whirlwind, doesn't it? A New Year's Eve wedding, all those tabloids catching wind of it..."

Before I could respond, she pivoted to Sam. "And, Sam, I think people would love to hear your side, too. Some of your fans were absolutely heartbroken when they found out," she added with a laugh, though her eyes sparkled with mischief. "Did you propose on a whim? Was this one of those 'love at first sight' situations?"

Sam chuckled, the sound a bit forced. "Not exactly. I've known Faye for a long time," he said, giving me a warm look that felt like an anchor in the rising tide of Amy's probing questions. "It's not something we planned to happen right now, but I'm glad it did."

Amy pounced, her smile sharpening even more. "So, you're saying it wasn't premeditated at all? That's interesting, especially considering the buzz around your recent hospital visit, Faye.

Some people are speculating there might have been... tension between you two following the wedding."

My stomach dropped. I could see where she was leading, twisting her phrasing in that carefully veiled way to plant seeds of doubt, as if she were hinting at some dark undercurrent between us.

"Well," she continued, feigning concern, "we're all curious, you know. It's not every day that a high-profile couple with such intense careers suddenly ties the knot, especially with rumours about a disagreement that ended with you in the hospital. I mean, no one's saying anything definitive, of course, but—"

"I'm going to stop you right there," I interrupted, fighting to control my anger. I leaned forward, my gaze fixed on Amy with a deadly calm. "I tripped and hit my head. Anyone suggesting otherwise clearly doesn't know Sam—or me—at all."

The atmosphere in the room shifted instantly, the temperature seeming to drop as a thick silence settled over us.

Amy's carefully rehearsed smile slipped, and I saw a flicker of uncertainty in her eyes as she tried to backpedal, her voice suddenly more hesitant. "Of course, of course, I only meant—"

"I know exactly what you meant," I said, my

voice like ice. "And to imply anything other than the truth of this matter is not only misinformation but potentially damaging to a man whom I love and admire." I placed my hand deliberately on Sam's knee.

Sam's fingers entwined with mine, squeezing.

"We understand the public interest in our relationship, and we respect that people want to know more about us," Sam slid in smoothly, sounding unreasonably calm and collected. "But we're here to talk about the tour. The band has worked hard on new material that we can't wait to share with fans."

Justice picked up the thread, talking enthusiastically about their new songs, but I could feel Sam's tension simmering beside me, see it in the tight line of his jaw and the way his hand stayed possessively on my shoulder.

Finally, the red light blinked off, signaling the end of the segment. Amy's apology was as shallow as her smile, and I responded with practiced politeness—despite my desire to tell her where to shove it. Sam kept an arm wrapped around my shoulder, his tension was like a live wire beside me, barely held in check.

As soon as we were clear of the studio and lost in the bustle of crew breaking down equipment, Sam grabbed my hand. "Come on."

"Sam—"

"Not here."

He pulled me toward the exit, weaving through the crowd until we reached the limo waiting outside, its dark, sleek lines reflecting the cool winter light. The driver opened the door, and I barely had time to climb inside before Sam followed, closing the door firmly behind him.

He hit the intercom button. "Drive."

"What about the others?" I protested, twisting in my seat to see them emerge from the station, stopping to sign merch for the multitude of fans that waited for them.

"They can get a fucking taxi."

I cocked one eyebrow. "What's up your nose? That went well."

"Well?" He stared at me from across the rear of the car. "Faye, you practically slapped her."

"I had it handled," I said, my frustration flaring. "She was baiting you, Sam. I needed to—"

"Handled?!" His harsh laugh cut ribbons through my heart. "If they want to accuse me of something, let them. I have nothing to hide."

"You're angry because I shut her down? It's my job to control these situations."

"I don't need you to defend me. And I'm not a fucking 'situation.'"

"Yes, you are!" I shot back, leaning forward, anger vibrating through every nerve. "We are! We're the very definition of situation-ship. What do you think I am if not a complication to be managed?"

"My wife!"

Shocked silence crackled between us, hot and heavy with frustration, resentment... and something else. Something that made my heart race in a way that had nothing to do with anger. His eyes searched mine, fierce and conflicted, his breathing shallow.

"Fuck it," he muttered, voice thick with frustration.

Before I could process what was happening, he closed the space between us, his mouth crashing into mine. For a split second, I froze, shocked by the feel of his lips on mine, the sheer heat behind it. But then something inside me snapped, and I was kissing him back just as fiercely, my hands fisting in his shirt, pulling him closer.

He groaned against my mouth, one hand sliding into my hair as the other gripped my hip, pulling me flush against him. This kiss wasn't the careful, staged peck we'd given for the cameras. This was raw, real, filled with every unspoken thing between us, every simmering argument, every unsaid word. His lips were hot, demanding, as he kissed me like he was claiming me, and I gave as good as I got, pouring my frustration and pent-up desire into every clash of our mouths.

After a breathless minute, he pulled back, chest heaving, his forehead resting against mine as he tried to catch his breath.

"Fuck, sorry." He started to pull away, but I wasn't having it.

I grabbed his shirt, yanking him back to me. "Don't you dare stop."

A spark of heat flared in his eyes, and he kissed me again, deeper this time, his hands slipping under my dress, tracing patterns up my thigh that made me shiver. My fingers worked at the buttons of his shirt, desperate to feel more, to get closer, as the world outside the limo faded away, leaving only the two of us tangled together in a feverish haze of need.

"Are you really angry?" I gasped as he kissed his way down my neck.

"Yes. I'm angry you defended me when all I wanted to do was kiss you and I had no fucking right." His head lifted, his lips capturing mine in a hungry, desperate kiss.

I moaned into his mouth, groaning as our tongues tangled, deep, hot and wet. He kissed like he was starving, desperate to devour me whole.

I liked it. A lot.

I barely registered as the car slowed to a stop. A faint knock on the privacy window shattered our spell. We both froze, breathing heavily, our bodies pressed together, chests rising and falling in sync. The driver cleared his throat from the other side of the partition.

"We've arrived," he called, voice muffled but unmistakably amused.

I looked at Sam, lips swollen, hair mussed from where my fingers had run through it. His eyes met mine, dark with desire and a trace of something else, something softer, like he couldn't believe what had just happened.

Reluctantly, he let his hands drop, adjusting his shirt with a rueful smile. "Guess we'll have to pick this up later."

"Guess so." I gave him a small, breathless smile.

"Faye, don't defend me unless you want to be kissed like that again." He ran his thumb over my lower lip. "I don't have it in me to resist you."

For a woman who built her life on words, I found myself suddenly speechless.

I stared at Sam, chest heaving, lips swollen from our frantic kiss. My skin tingled everywhere he'd touched me, and his words, *"I don't have it in me to resist you,"* played on loop in my head.

What the fuck? What the actual fuck?

I scrambled, trying to slot this into some logical framework. We'd been arguing, practically spitting fire at each other, and then he'd kissed me. No—*we* had kissed, and not some safe, chaste kiss like we'd planned for the cameras. This was raw, consuming, everything I'd been holding back, everything I'd told myself I wasn't allowed to feel. I had never felt so stripped bare, so exposed.

I didn't know how to process the mess of emotions swirling inside me. I raised my fingertips to my lips, a shiver of disbelief at the way he'd kissed me rocketing down my spine.

He'd kissed me like he was claiming me, branding me. And the most terrifying part? I'd wanted him to. I'd been all in, letting myself sink into that moment, giving as good as I got.

I glanced at him, adjusting his shirt beside me with that maddening half smile, and felt the urge to reach out, to pull him back to me, to taste him again, consequences be damned. But this time, it wasn't just lust or attraction; it was the weight of everything we'd been through, every unspoken word, every quiet night working late, every time he'd known what I needed before I'd even asked. And it felt too big, too real, to keep at arm's length any longer.

This is insane, I told myself, forcing a deep breath. *He's your best friend. Don't complicate this.*

But I couldn't help but remember the way he'd looked at me, that fierce, unguarded intensity in his gaze, the way he'd called me his wife like it meant something—like he wanted it to mean something.

"Ready?" he asked, one hand on the door.

"I..." I hesitated, searching for some way to brush this off, to keep things simple. To kill the emotions we'd awakened. But the words died on my tongue.

I sucked in a breath, nodding silently.

Subdued, we climbed out of the limo and re-entered the real world, but I knew we'd crossed a line. One that wouldn't be easily uncrossed.

Damn.

6

SAM

*- The Wild Ones, "The Way She
Moves"*

~

The problem with kissing someone you've wanted for years is that once you've had a taste, you can't think about anything else.

I watched Faye move through the pre-show chaos, all professional efficiency in her fitted black dress, tablet in hand as she coordinated last-minute details. She hadn't met my eyes since the limo incident, but I couldn't stop watching her—the graceful line of her neck, the way she bit her lower lip when concentrating, how her hands moved as she directed the crew.

The same hands that had been tangled in my hair just hours ago.

"Earth to Sam." Justice waved a hand in front of my face. "Your guitar's out of tune."

"What? Oh." I looked down at my hands, realizing I'd been absently plucking the same string for who knows how long. "Sorry."

"You okay?" He lowered his voice, glancing between Faye and me. "You've been weird since the interview."

I started to retune my guitar, grateful for something to focus on besides the memory of Faye's body pressed against mine. "I'm fine."

"You sure? Amy went pretty hard on you."

I shrugged. "Not unexpected. And Faye handled it."

Justice leaned against a tower of speakers, crossing his arms. "Ah, that explains it."

I cocked an eyebrow in question.

"Why you're staring at Faye like she's water in the desert."

"I haven't been—"

"Sam!" Faye's call cut through the noise. She hadn't glanced up from her iPad, determinedly avoiding my gaze. "The label wants photos before the show. Can you...?" She gestured vaguely toward the backdrop they'd set up.

"Whatever you need." The words came out huskier than intended.

Her cheeks darkened slightly as her eyes finally met mine for a brief, electric moment before skittering away. She turned quickly, but not before I caught the flash of something in her gaze.

Good. At least I wasn't the only one affected.

The next hour passed in a blur of preparations, both of us dancing around each other like magnets with reverse polarity. Every time she came near, my skin buzzed with awareness. Every accidental brush of hands felt like lightning.

"Here." She appeared at my elbow as I finished my warmup, holding out my bucket of spare guitar picks. "You left these in the greenroom."

I took it, our fingers touching briefly. The contact sent electricity shooting up my arm. "Thanks."

She started to turn away, but I caught her wrist. "Faye—"

"Don't." Her voice was soft, almost pleading. "We have a show to do."

"And after?"

She finally met my eyes, and the heat there nearly knocked me back.

"We'll talk," she agreed, then pulled away, already speaking into her headset about camera angles and lighting.

I watched her go, remembering how she'd felt in my arms, the little sounds she'd made when I'd kissed her neck, the way she'd pulled me closer instead of pushing me away.

"Dude." Felix appeared beside me, following my gaze. "You've got it bad."

"Shut up and tune your bass."

He grinned, unrepentant. "Just saying, for a fake marriage, you guys look pretty real to me."

I thought about Faye's hands fisted in my shirt, her breathless "Don't you dare stop," the way she'd kissed me back like she'd been wanting it as much as I had.

"Five minutes!" the stage manager called. "Places, everyone!"

I strapped on my guitar, trying to focus on

the show ahead and not on the memory of Faye's body pressed against mine in the back of that limo.

We'll talk, she'd said.

I intended to hold her to that promise.

The crowd roared as the lights dimmed, the opening band closing out their set with a rousing number.

As the stage went dark and we ran on, I forced myself to focus on the music. In place, I glanced around, waiting for the nod from my band mates before my fingers strummed the opening chords.

The crowd went wild, screaming a wave of sound toward the stage. It raised goose bumps on my skin, and had Justice chuckling from somewhere to my left.

But all I could think about was how Faye's lips had felt against mine, and how much I wanted to kiss her again.

Later. After. Soon.

Finally.

The final chord of our set rang out through the arena, sweat dripping down my back as the crowd roared. Three and a half hours of playing, two encores and a third standing ovation had me exhausted but pumped up on adrenaline.

As Justice thanked the crowd, I finally

allowed myself to look toward the wings where I knew she'd be waiting. Faye stood in her usual spot, iPad forgotten in her hands as she watched us.

But she wasn't alone.

Alex leaned against the wall beside her, too close for comfort, his perfectly tailored suit a stark contrast to our post-show sweat-drenched chaos. Even from here, I could see the tension in Faye's shoulders, the way she angled her body away from him while maintaining professional politeness.

"Great show," Alex said as we filed offstage, his voice carrying that practiced smoothness that set my teeth on edge. "The energy was electric."

"Always is," I muttered darkly, shooting him a glare as I made my way to Faye. Slinging an arm around her shoulders, I leaned in nuzzling her hair. "You okay?"

"Peachy," she said through gritted teeth. "But I'll survive."

We walked down to the greenroom, accepting congratulations and thanking our crew as we walked. Inside were the VIPs. We'd do an hour of meet and greet before finally being allowed to head back to the bus.

I held the door open for Faye but Alex stopped me before we could enter.

"You guys go ahead," he told Radley, Felix, and Justice. "I need to talk to the newlyweds for a moment."

Felix caught my eye, cocking his head.

"Go in," I murmured. "We'll be a minute."

Faye stepped beside me, her hand finding mine as we waited for them to file past. The door bumped shut, leaving us in the semi-dark of the hallway.

Alex crossed his arms, his expression patronizing.

"We have a problem."

Faye's hand flexed in mine.

I clenched my jaw, barely holding back the impulse to knock that smug look off Alex's face. He had that infuriating air of superiority, the way he held himself, like he was always a few steps above the rest of us. But what set my teeth on edge the most was how close he was to Faye, cornering her with his words, like he knew exactly where to dig, exactly which scars to press his fingers into.

Not on my watch.

"And that is?" I prompted.

"The label's been doing some digging." Alex pulled out his phone, his smile sharp. "Interesting what you find when you look hard enough. Like old yearbook photos from Capricorn Cove High." He looked up, eyes glinting. "You two were quite close back then, weren't you?"

Faye stiffened beside me. "That was years ago."

"Was it?" Alex scrolled through his phone. "Because according to these photos, you were quite... friendly. Theatre club, band, debate team, and this is just what we found today." He looked between us. "Yet somehow that connection never made it into any of your employment paperwork when you signed the label's contract."

My fingers twitched, my pulse thundering in my ears. He was baiting her, trying to unnerve her, using anything he could to make her doubt herself, to paint her as if she was just some opportunist using me to climb the ladder. It was the same tactic he'd used years ago, the same methodical, calculated way he'd dismantled her career one whisper at a time. And I knew, just by looking at him, he wouldn't stop until he saw her break.

Not this time.

"It wasn't relevant," Faye said, her voice firm and calm but for the slight tremor of tension. "No one ever asked."

"Wasn't it?" Alex's mouth curved into a smug smile, his eyes flicking to me, then back to her, a predator circling its prey. "From where

I'm standing, it looks an awful lot like you leveraged a personal connection for professional gain." His smile turned cruel. "Just like you did at Preston & Myers."

The rage that had been simmering beneath my skin boiled over. My free hand clenched into a fist at my side, every muscle in my body tensing as his words hit like a slap. Faye's face had gone pale, her hand gripping mine with a desperation I hadn't felt from her before, and seeing her like that—vulnerable, trying to keep it together as he tore into her—was the last straw.

"That's not—" she started, but Alex cut her off.

"I'm stating facts. The label has concerns about your potential conflicts of interest and about the integrity of certain employment decisions."

"But—"

Alex cut her off, stepping closer, feeding off her uncertainty, her pain. And something in me snapped.

"Faye, I think you need to resi—"

My fist connected with the wall beside his head before I even realized I'd moved. "Choose your next words very carefully."

Alex flinched, his smile faltering.

"Sam." Faye's hand on my arm was gentle but firm. "Sam, stop. He's not worth it."

I released him slowly, stepping back to Faye's side. Alex straightened his suit, that smug smile still in place.

"The label wants a full investigation into any potential impropriety. Starting with your initial hiring." He adjusted his cuffs. "Unless, of course, Faye prefers to resign. Save everyone the embarrassment."

I felt my pulse hammering in my ears. He had no idea what he was talking about—no idea what Faye had been through, what she'd sacrificed, what she'd done to rebuild her life after he'd torn it apart. And to stand here, to accuse her of using me, of somehow scheming her way into this job, after all the years she'd spent busting her ass for us? It was too much.

"Shut the fuck up. You don't know a damn thing about us," I said, my voice low and deadly, barely keeping my temper in check. "She's been with this band since day one. She's done more for us than you or anyone else at that label ever has."

Alex smirked, clearly unbothered by my anger. In fact, he looked downright pleased, like he'd been waiting for me to lose control. "And isn't that convenient? All thanks to that old 'friendship' from high school. What a fairy-tale story for the fans," he sneered.

The room felt like it was spinning, my vision tunneling as his words sank in. Every insult he hurled felt like a punch, aimed directly at Faye, at the very core of who she was, and I couldn't take it. I couldn't stand the thought of him tearing her down, of him dredging up her past, twisting our history into something ugly and cheap.

"We'll need to arrange a time for a formal sit-down—"

"That won't be necessary."

We all turned to find Justice standing in the doorway, arms crossed.

"I hired Faye," he continued, moving to stand beside us. "After she saved our asses at that charity event where our previous manager got wasted and spouted some racist shit."

I remembered that night. Faye had stepped in, handled the press, smoothed over ruffled feathers, and somehow turned the whole thing into positive publicity. It had occurred just as the label had come courting—and her quick actions had saved us from being relegated into the junk pile of obscurity.

"Sam didn't even know she was interviewing," Justice added.

Alex's smile slipped slightly. "That doesn't change—"

"What it changes," Justice cut in, "is your whole narrative. Any other accusations you'd like me to destroy? Or should we discuss how the label might react when they learn their new crisis manager is trying to fabricate scandals?"

For the first time, Alex looked uncertain.

"You know what your problem is, Alex?" Faye's voice was steady now, stronger. "You see manipulation everywhere because that's all you know how to do. But some of us actually earn our success."

"I'm just doing my job." His smile was sharp. "Making sure everything stays... professional. We wouldn't want anyone making decisions they might regret. Again."

Faye flinched. It was tiny, barely noticeable, but I felt it where our arms touched.

"We're done here," I ground out, my voice rough, barely controlled. "You don't get to talk to my wife like that. Not now, not fucking ever. You come near her again and you better fucking believe there will be consequences." I held my hand out. "Faye?"

She took my hand, allowing me to lead her away, but Alex's voice stopped us.

"Have a good night, you two," he called after us. "But not *too* good."

She froze beside me, and I saw the flash of annoyance cross her face.

"Alex," she said sweetly over her shoulder. "Go fuck yourself."

I guided her through the backstage chaos toward the exit. She didn't resist, letting me lead her out into the cool night air and toward the waiting tour bus.

I pulled my cell out of my pocket as we walked, barely containing the rage simmering under my skin.

"Sam! To what do I owe this call?" Hendrix Archer, the CEO of the parent company of record label answered immediately.

"Hendrix, sorry to call you so late but I have a problem."

I glanced down at Faye, catching her frowning up at me.

"Well let's see if we can't fix it. What's the issue?"

"The label has sent a guy to sort out the apparent mess my marriage has caused. Let's be honest, Hendrix, there is no mess. Sales are up, our name is splashed across the media, and Faye is gem. I want Alex Pontiff gone. Faye and Liz can handle this. And I will not tolerate the disrespect this fucking guy is showing my wife."

Faye's hand tightened in mine as I guided us toward the bus.

"I understand and you're right. I'll take care of it."

"Appreciate that."

"Have a good rest of your night, Sam. And best wishes to you and Faye."

"Thanks."

I hung up, guiding Faye into the bus with a gentle hand on her lower back.

The familiar interior welcomed us, quiet and empty—the rest of the band looking after the VIPs and press for at least another hour. I followed her into the small kitchen area, watching as she sank onto one of the benches.

"Want to talk about it?"

She stared at her hands, still clutched together in her lap. "Not really."

"Okay." I moved to the tiny kitchen, pulling out two mugs. "Tea?"

A small smile tugged at her lips. "You don't have to take care of me. I'm not the one who punched a wall."

I needed to do something with my hands— the anger still sizzled in my blood.

"I wish it had been his face." I set the kettle to boil, leaning against the counter to face her. "But I also want to understand why seeing him hurts you so much."

She was quiet for a long moment, fidgeting with the hem of her dress. Finally, she looked up, meeting my eyes. "When he did what he did, he didn't just steal my work, Sam. He stole my confidence. Made me doubt everything about myself—my judgment, my professionalism, my ability to separate personal from business."

"And now?"

"Now he's here, watching, waiting for me to mess up again." Her laugh was bitter. "Maybe I already have."

I crossed to her, kneeling in front of her bench so she had to look at me. "Hey. You haven't messed up anything."

"Haven't I?" Her eyes searched mine. "Our marriage, that kiss…"

"Was perfect," I finished. "And I'd very much like to do it again. But only when you're ready."

Surprise flickered across her face. "You're serious?"

"Deadly." I took her hands in mine, enjoying how perfectly we fit together. "Not to be dismissive but you're a fucking great kisser."

She stared at our joined hands, then back at me. "I… you are too."

I grinned. "I know."

She kicked me.

"Look, as much as I want to kiss you, I'm also okay if we stay exactly as we are. Friends, partners, whatever you need." I squeezed her fingers gently. "But I hope you'll give us a chance. When you're ready."

The kettle whistled, breaking the moment. I stood, reluctantly letting go of her hands to fix our tea.

"Sam?"

"Hmm?"

"I'll think about it."

I turned back to her, finding her watching me with soft eyes. "Yeah?"

She nodded. "Yeah. Just... give me time?"

"All you need." I handed her a mug of peppermint tea, then settled onto the bench opposite. "Though I should warn you, I might stare at you a lot. And think about kissing you. Probably write some embarrassingly romantic songs."

She snorted and we settled into comfortable silence, sipping our tea and stealing glances at each other across the small space. Eventually, exhaustion caught up with me.

"Gonna head to bed."

"I should too."

We headed up to the sleeping area, swapping between the bathroom as we quietly got ready for bed.

"Goodnight, Sam," she said softly, climbing into her bunk.

"Goodnight, Faye."

I lay in my bunk opposite hers, watching as she settled in, her silk bonnet already in place. She caught me looking and smiled—a real smile, soft and sweet and just for me.

"Sam?"

"Yeah?"

"That kiss really was perfect."

I grinned into the darkness. "Just wait until the next one."

Her quiet laugh followed me into sleep, and for the first time since this whole marriage thing started, I felt truly hopeful.

I fell asleep watching her through half-closed eyes, memorizing the way she looked in the dim light of the bus.

I'd wait. She was worth it.

7

FAYE

FAMILY GROUP CHAT RISK ASSESSMENT

Priority Level: HIGH
Status: WHAT IS HAPPENING???????

IMMEDIATE OBSERVATIONS
☐ Added to "Dogg Pack" group text
☐ 147 unread messages and counting
☐ Multiple gif usage
☐ Excessive emojis
☐ Sam's dad posts dad jokes hourly
Note: SAVE FAVORITES FOR LATER

CURRENT CONCERNS:

- Everyone types in ALL CAPS

- Jay keeps sending awkward selfies
- Frankie's "relationship" memes
- Will's dad jokes are actually funny
- Sam watching me read with a grin

Note: STOP NOTICING SAM'S GRIN

EMERGENCY PROTOCOLS

- Read but don't respond
- Selective emoji usage
- Maintain professional distance
- Try not to get attached

Note: TOO LATE???

Current Status: Information overload
Threat Level: INCREASING

Personal Note: Why does this feel so natural?

Secondary Note: These people are chaos

Final Note: I might love it

~

My phone buzzed for the hundredth time that morning, another notification from the "Dogg Pack" family chat lighting up my screen.

DOGG PACK CHAT
DADDYDOGG

WHY DON'T EGGS TELL JOKES?

MOMMYDOGG

Please don't...

DADDYDOGG

THEY'D CRACK UP!

MR.JAYKENTON

Dad, no. Please stop.

FRANKIEKENTON

Keep 'em coming, Will!

MOMMYDOGG

Will's been saving these up all
week. You're just lucky they're
egg jokes and not wedding jokes.
I'm looking at you @SamDogg
and @FayeMoyo.

SAMDOGG

Sorry @FayeMoyo, you can mute
them if you want

I glanced up from my phone to find Sam
watching me from across the tour bus kitchen,
amusement dancing in his eyes as he sipped his
morning tea.

"Your family is chaos," I informed him, even
as I saved Will's joke to my growing collection.

"Our family now," he corrected. "At least
according to Karen's latest text."

As if on cue, my phone buzzed again.

MOMMYDOGG

@FAYEMOYO HONEY WHEN
ARE YOU COMING FOR
DINNER?

MOMMYDOGG

Sorry, I hit caps. You know, none
of you visit enough. When was
the last time we all had dinner
together?

JAMESDOGG

Thanksgiving. We literally were all together for thanksgiving.

MOMMYDOGG

But we missed Christmas! Sam was away and Hayden and Kat had to take the kids to London to visit her parents. I miss you all!

LITTLEDOGG

I don't.

MOMMYDOGG

Ignore your sister. She's annoyed that she has to go back to school next week.

DADDYDOGG

WHY DID THE SCARECROW WIN AN AWARD?

DADDYDOGG

BECAUSE HE WAS OUTSTANDING IN HIS FIELD!

MR.JAYKENTON

Speaking of dinner...

FRANKIEKENTON

••••••

MR.JAYKENTON

Frankie and I are happy to host if you guys want to come over. @SamDogg, you're gig free tonight, right? And only an hour and a half drive away. See? Perfect!

FRANKIEKENTON

Is it? Seems like a lot of work for them.

FRANKIEKENTON

I mean, Yes! Faye, we need girl talk!

HAZELDOGG

We're in – I'll make dessert

MILLIEDOGG

I'll make sure we're free. I can bring a salad.

ASHDOGG

I thought we had a work thing tonight?

MILLIEDOGG

I'll move it. I don't want to miss Faye's initiation dinner.

TRENTMOYO-DOGG

Welcome to the fam, sis! Be
prepared for the unexpected.
Seriously, I found a snake in our
house last week after someone
came over.

JAMESDOGG

I PLEAD THE FIFTH!!!!

RYANDOGG-MOYO

Don't scare her! We need
someone in the family who'll rope
our chaos in.

ENIDTENIL

Henry and I are a yes—we'll bring
wine.

KATDOGG

Party!!

Sam set down his mug, crossing to where
I sat.

"We don't have to go if you're not up for it."

I looked at him, noting the careful way he
asked, like he was trying not to pressure me.

"You want to go?"

He shrugged, but I caught the tension in his
shoulders. "It'd be nice to see them. And we are
only an hour and a half away."

"Then we'll go." I turned back to my phone,
typing quickly.

FAYEMOYO

We'll be there. What can we bring?

FRANKIEKENTON

Just yourselves! And maybe some juicy stories about married life 😈

MR.JAYKENTON

Frankie, no. I draw a line.

FRANKIEKENTON

I didn't say you had to be a part of the conversation

SAMDOGG

And on that note, I'm muting this chat. We'll see you tonight.

ASHDOGG

Coward

RYANDOGG-MOYO

You can't escape the dad jokes, Samuel. Embrace them.
EMBRACE THEM!!!

I couldn't help laughing, even as my phone continued to buzz with notifications.

Sam's hand settled on my shoulder. "You sure about dinner? The family can be... intense."

I chuckled. "I have met your family before.

You know, on account of your brother being married to mine. It's not like I'm going in cold. I can handle them."

A thump came on the side of the bus. "Sound check in five!"

Sam's thumb brushed the base of my neck, sending shivers down my spine.

"Alright, but don't say I didn't warn you." He squeezed my shoulders before moving toward the bus door.

I stood, following him out. "How bad could it possibly be?"

He chuckled. "You have no idea."

"You're overthinking again." Sam's voice drifted from the bathroom of the bus where he was changing. "I can hear you from here."

"I am not." I straightened his leather jacket on its hanger, checking for wrinkles. "I'm just..."

"Making sure everything's perfect?"

"It's dinner with your family."

"What happened to 'I can handle them'?" he teased, emerging in dark jeans and a soft gray Henley that made something flutter in my stomach.

"Yes, well normally I could. But this isn't

exactly normal. We've kind of... you know..." I gestured between us.

"Shacked up?"

Heat crept up my neck. "Exactly. What if they can tell we're faking it?"

Sam crossed to where I stood, gently taking his jacket from my hands. "Faye, breathe."

"I am breathing."

"No, you're spiraling." He shrugged into the jacket, and I absolutely did not notice how it pulled across his shoulders. "Everyone just wants to see us. No agenda."

"No agenda," I echoed dubiously.

"It'll be fine." Sam's hand found the small of my back, guiding me toward the steps. "Though fair warning, Frankie's probably going to ask about our sex life."

I stumbled. "She what?"

"Sexologist, remember?" His grin was far too amused. "She likes to make people squirm with inappropriate questions. It's her love language."

"And you're just reminding me of this now?"

"Would you have agreed to go if I'd told you earlier?"

"No!"

"Exactly." He pressed the open door button on the bus, waiting for the exit doors to slide open. "Besides, you're the one who's always saying we need to make this look real."

I narrowed my eyes at him. "I hate you."

"No, you don't."

As we stepped out onto the grass lot, Sam's phone buzzed.

"Justice wants to know if we'll be back in time for an early rehearsal tomorrow."

"Tell him yes. We need to run through the new arrangement for 'Wild Heart' before tomorrow's show." I frowned as a thought hit me. "Unless... do you want to stay longer with your family? I can handle rehearsal notes—"

"Faye." Sam's voice was soft. "Stop trying to manage everything."

"I'm not—" I caught his knowing look. "Fine. But someone has to."

"And someone has to make sure you don't work yourself to death." He bumped my shoulder with his. "Good thing you married me."

My heart did that strange flutter again.

"Car's here," Sam said, nodding to where our driver waited. His hand found my lower back again, warm and steady. "Ready?"

I thought about Frankie's inappropriate questions, about Jay's cryptic text, about how natural Sam's touch felt.

"Not even slightly."

He laughed, the sound wrapping around me like a familiar melody. "That's my girl."

And for just a moment, I let myself believe he meant it.

I slid into the back seat, only to be immediately assaulted by memories of the last time we'd been alone in the back of a limo.

Flushing, I ducked my head, pulling my phone out of my bag to text Hope.

FAYEMOYO

911!! HELP!!!

HOPE

Did he kiss you again??????

FAYEMOYO

No, but we've returned to the scene of the crime. And I am NOT ready to go down that path.

HOPE

Why not? He's hot, you're technically married / single. Get it girl!

FAYEMOYO

You are not being helpful...

HOPE

I'm a virgin who writes steamy romance. Cut me some slack. I need to live vicariously through you

During the hour and a bit car ride, I attempted to distract myself with emails and phone calls—anything other than glancing at Sam.

There lay danger...

Jay and Frankie's house sat in the middle of the small town of Capricorn Cove, a modern single-story bungalow that had been carefully upgraded to include wheelchair access and additional rooms. Warm light spilled from the windows, and the smell of something delicious wafted from inside out across the lawn.

A lawn that was strewn with dinosaurs.

It was a Jay thing, apparently.

"Finally!" Frankie called as she opened the door, her wheelchair expertly maneuvering back to let us in. Her pink hair was styled in a fashionable high ponytail, her smile knowing as she looked between us. "I was starting to think you'd gotten lost—or maybe pulled over for a quickie."

"Frankie," Jay's warning tone came from the kitchen.

"What? I'm just saying they have that newlywed glow."

I fought back a blush as Sam leaned down to hug her. "Missed you too, Frankie."

"Of course you did. I'm delightful." She

turned her chair toward me, arms open. "Come here, gorgeous. Let me see this ring."

As I bent to hug her, she whispered, "Welcome to the family."

Before I could respond, Jay appeared, wiping his hands on a dish towel.

"Rainbow, at least get them a drink before pumping them for all the juicy details," he told Frankie, pulling Sam into a bear hug. "Hey, bro."

"As a professional—" Frankie started to protest.

"You're not getting paid to analyze us," Sam cut in smoothly.

"No, but you're family. I'll do it for you guys for free."

I laughed despite my nerves.

"Something smells amazing," I said, trying to redirect the conversation.

"Jay's making his famous pasta." Frankie headed toward the kitchen. "Come help me set the table while these two do their brooding man-chat thing."

"We don't brood," Jay and Sam said simultaneously.

"Sure, you don't." Frankie winked at me. "The rest of the family are out back."

I followed her to the dining room, hearing voices drifting from the back porch.

Something about football and endless possibilities.

Jay and Frankie's house had once been a small beach bungalow but at some point, Jay had blown out the rear of the property to expand it into a full indoor/outdoor living area. In summer, all the doors and windows could be left open, inviting in the warm sea breeze. While on days like today when winter had settled into your bones and snow piled on the ground, the triple-glazed storm glass was closed tight, sealing us into a warm, cozy house.

"They're here!"

I wasn't sure who called out, but in the next instance we were swarmed by both Sam's family and—surprisingly—my own.

"Dad? Mom?"

"Baby!" My mother, Nora, wrapped me in her arms, pulling me tight against her. "You're too thin. Are you eating enough on tour?"

"She is," Sam answered before I could, accepting a handshake from my father. "I make sure of it."

"Good man," my dad said, clapping Sam on the shoulder. "Though you couldn't have waited for us to be at the wedding?"

"Chidi," my mother scolded. "They're young and in love. Sometimes these things just happen."

I caught Sam's eye over my mother's shoulder, finding him fighting a grin.

"Speaking of the wedding," Karen, Sam's adopted mom said, swooping in to steal me from my mother's arms. "Will and I are thinking we could throw you a renewal ceremony. Something small, intimate..."

"With proper planning this time," Will added, ruffling Sam's hair as he passed. "Though I have to admit, the unicorn celebrant was a nice touch."

"I need a drink," I muttered.

"Way ahead of you," my brother called from the kitchen. "Wine's breathing." He walked in holding a bunch of glasses in his hands. "Mom wants to discuss the sleeping arrangements for Christmas."

"It's January," Sam said, exchanging another glance with me.

"Exactly! Only eleven months to plan!" Karen linked arms with my mother. "Nora and I were thinking we could try James's lake house?"

"Don't drag me into this!" James protested from his spot beside Hazel on the couch.

"Or we could all rent a ski cabin," my mother countered. "Somewhere the whole family can stay together."

"Ash is thinking of buying one," Millie said from where she stood with her husband, attempting to soothe a screaming toddler. "Right, babe?"

"Um, sure," he said, wincing as a small fist flew against his chest.

"The whole family meaning...?" I asked warily.

"Us," Mom said, making an all-encompassing gesture.

"Great," Sam muttered.

"I need a drink," I announced again to no one in particular.

As if on cue, Sam appeared at my side, pressing a glass of wine into my hand.

"Breathe," he murmured against my ear. "They're just teasing."

"They're planning our future," I whispered back.

"Is that such a bad thing?" Something in his tone made me look up. His eyes were soft, uncertain in a way I rarely saw.

Before I could respond, Jay called everyone to dinner. We were herded toward the massive dining table, somehow ending up wedged between our mothers, who were already deep in discussion about holiday traditions and whose turn it would be to host Thanksgiving next year.

"Faye," Frankie called. "Can you help me with plates?"

Grateful for any excuse to escape this weird Brady Bunch-esque cult moment, I hurried after her into the sanctuary of the quiet kitchen.

"So," Frankie said as she handed me plates from a low cabinet. "How are you really doing?"

"I'm—"

...overwhelmed, exhausted, overstimulated, confused, horny...

"—fine."

"Hmm." She watched me arrange the plates with precise movements, lining them up one by one in a tall stack. "You know what I love about my job?"

"Making people uncomfortable with sex talk?"

She laughed, handing me a final plate. "Besides that. I love that I get to help people be honest with themselves."

I set down the plate harder than necessary. "Frankie..."

"You know what I see when I look at you and Sam?"

"Two people managing a complicated situation professionally?"

"Two people who are so afraid of losing what they have, they can't see what they could have, what they want and need."

I felt that like a gut punch. "It's not like that."

"No?" She moved to the wine rack, selecting a bottle. "Then why do you keep straightening those plates?"

I looked down to find I'd been obsessively adjusting the table settings. "I just like things to be right."

"Some things don't need to be perfect to be right." She handed me the wine. "They just need to be real."

Before I could respond, Sam's laugh drifted in from outside. The sound wrapped around me like a familiar song, and I found myself smiling automatically.

"See?" Frankie's voice was gentle. "Real."

"It's complicated."

"Love usually is." She headed back toward the rowdy group. "Doesn't make it less worth it."

I watched her go, her words settling uncomfortably in my chest. Because the thing was, I'd noticed changes lately.

The way Sam's touch lingered.

The way his songs seemed to hit differently.

The way I found myself turning to him first, with everything.

But noticing feelings and acting on them were very different things.

Weren't they?

"Hey." Sam appeared in the doorway. "You

okay? You've been staring at that wine bottle for a while."

I looked down at the bottle still clutched in my hands. "Just thinking."

"Dangerous pastime."

"For you, maybe."

His laugh was soft as he crossed to me, taking the wine. "Come on. Jay's about to serve, he has a whole thing about cold pasta—no one wants to be subjected to that rant."

"Sam?"

"Hmm?"

"Are we..." I hesitated, not sure what I was asking. *Are we okay? Are we real? Are we making a mistake?*

His free hand found mine, squeezing gently. "We're good, Faye. Promise."

And the thing was, I believed him.

Even if I wasn't sure what "good" meant anymore.

Dinner was exactly as chaotic as I should have expected from this family.

Jay told stories about the lumber yard between bites of pasta, while Frankie interrupted with increasingly inappropriate questions about tour life. Kids ran riot around the table while babies cried and were passed around to whoever had a free hand.

Sam kept his hand on my knee under the

table, a gesture that was probably meant to be reassuring but instead, sent sparks up my spine every time he moved.

"So," Frankie said, refilling my wine glass with a worrying gleam in her eye. "Tell us about the wedding night."

I choked on my pasta.

"Frankie," Jay warned.

"What? It's a valid question. I mean, they went from friends to married. That's a big jump. There had to be some underlying tension there."

Sam's hand tightened on my knee. "We're not discussing our sex life."

"Who said anything about sex?" Frankie's smile was wicked. "I'm talking about emotional intimacy. The way long-time friends suddenly have to navigate new boundaries. The shift from professional to personal. Though if you want to talk about sex—"

"We don't," I cut in quickly.

"Spoilsports." She turned to Jay. "Babe, remember when we first got together? All that delicious tension from—"

"And that's enough wine for you." Jay smoothly moved the bottle away from his wife.

Heat crept up my neck. "Excuse me." I stood abruptly. "Bathroom?"

"Down the hall, second door on the right," Jay said.

I felt Sam's concerned gaze follow me as I fled—because that's what this was, wasn't it? Running from truths I wasn't ready to face.

The bathroom was all sleek lines and adaptive fixtures, a perfect blend of style and function, just like everything about Jay and Frankie's life together. I braced my hands on the sink, staring at my reflection.

"Get it together," I whispered to myself. "It's not real."

Except...

That kiss had been real. Our laughter, our easy teasing, the way he'd looked at me when he'd admitted he wanted to kiss me again.

The way he defended me, supported me, saw me... that was real.

Wasn't it?

A soft knock interrupted my spiral.

"Faye?" Will asked. "You okay in there?"

I opened the door to find him leaning against the wall, arms crossed, expression gentle.

"Sorry. I just needed a minute."

"I get it. It can be overwhelming." He tilted his head to one side. "But you're used to crowds. So that's not it."

I huffed out a laugh, mimicking his pose in

the doorway of the bathroom. "I don't know what it is. I just feel..."

"Untethered?"

Oof. Right in the feels.

I shrugged. "Maybe?"

"You know, it's okay to be scared. Marriage is a big commitment."

I bit my tongue to keep from admitting the truth.

"But I'm gonna let you in on a secret. As much as you're worried, Sam will be ten times as concerned. The fact is, he doesn't know his own worth. Never has. Probably never will, unless someone shows him."

My throat felt tight. "I don't—"

"You do." He smiled. "You see him. Really see him. Not the rock star, not the quiet helper, but Sam. And he sees you too. The real you, not just the perfect professional image you project."

"Will..."

"I know what it's like to be afraid of wanting things. To think you don't deserve them." He straightened. "But sometimes the best things in life are the ones you think you can't have."

"It's complicated."

"In my experience, love always is." He grinned. "But it's worth it."

Geeze. What was it with this family tonight?

Before I could respond, Sam's laugh drifted

down the hallway, followed by Frankie's delighted cackling.

My chest ached. "Why are you telling me this?"

"Because you're family too, Faye. Marriage certificate or not." He squeezed my shoulder. "Maybe it's time you both stopped pretending otherwise."

I stood in the hallway long after he left, listening to the sounds of my family—because they were all mine now, weren't they?—and wondering when exactly I'd lost control of this situation.

When I'd lost control of my heart.

"Oh," I whispered to no one. "Oh no."

Because that's what this feeling was, wasn't it?

That's what it had been all along.

Love.

8

SAM

- The Wild Ones, "Coded"

The drive back was too quiet.

Faye hadn't said more than two words since her talk with my dad, her fingers tapping restless patterns on her knee. I knew that look, had seen it countless times before shows or press conferences. It meant her mind was working overtime, trying to control something that scared her.

"They liked having you there," I said, testing the waters.

"Hmm."

"Frankie's already planning Sunday dinners when we're in town."

"That's nice."

I watched her reflection in the car window, the city lights painting shadows across her face. "She also suggested we should start a nudist colony."

"Uh-huh."

"And offer skidoo rentals."

"Sounds good."

"With free puppies for the first five hundred members."

"That's a good ide—wait, what?" She finally looked at me.

"There she is." I smiled. "Want to tell me what's going on in that head of yours?"

"Nothing." Too quick. Too sharp.

Liar.

"Faye."

"Sam." She mimicked my tone, but I caught the slight tremor in her voice.

I slid into the seat next to her, gently brushing her cheek with my knuckles. "You can tell me. Let me take some of the weight off your shoulders."

Her gaze raked across my face, her dark eyes flashing with some yet-to-be-expressed emotion.

"I don't want to talk."

Disappointed, I made a move to lean back, only to have her stop me with her next, devastating words.

"I want you to kiss me."

I froze, searching her face for any sign of hesitation or doubt. "Are you sure?"

I knew that once I crossed this line with her, there'd be no going back. No way I could pretend I didn't want her, didn't *need* her like this. I'd kept my distance for so long, telling myself it was for the best, that she deserved better, that what we had was good enough. But every time she was near, that thin resolve chipped away, bit by bit.

"I'm tired of being scared," she whispered, her fingers curling into my shirt. "Tired of pretending I don't want this. Want you."

I traced my thumb across her bottom lip, watching her eyes darken. "But if we do this, there's no going back. No pretending it didn't happen."

"I don't want to go back." Her voice was soft but certain. "I want to go forward. With you."

Something inside me broke free—all the longing, all the careful distance I'd maintained. God, she had no idea. She had no idea how long I'd been carrying this, how deep these feelings ran. It had started as a crush, simple and harmless, but as the years passed, it grew into something so fierce, so constant, that it became part of who I was.

I cradled her face in my hands, giving her one last chance to pull away.

Instead, she surged forward, pressing her lips to mine.

This kiss was different from our first. That had been heat and frustration, raw need bursting free This was deeper, slower, something profound and electric that spread through me like wildfire. I kissed her with every ounce of restraint I'd ever held, letting her feel the years of quiet longing, the nights I'd spent replaying the sound of her laughter, imagining what it would be like to touch her, to hold her like this.

Her hands slid into my hair as she shifted onto my lap, her body fitting against mine. She sighed against my mouth, a soft, contented sound that made my heart ache. I wanted to memorize everything about this moment—the way her lips moved with mine, the softness of her skin, the warmth of her body against mine.

I wanted to savor it, to take my time, because I'd waited so damn long for this, and I didn't want to miss a single second.

I traced kisses down her neck, breathing in the familiar scent of her perfume mixed with something uniquely Faye.

"Sam," she sighed, the sound sending sparks down my spine.

I could never go back to just being her friend. I couldn't pretend I hadn't felt this, hadn't tasted the way she said my name, sighing it like it meant something more. Like *I* meant something more.

I caught her lips again, pouring every unspoken word, every quiet moment I'd spent wanting her, into that kiss. I wanted her to know that this wasn't new, wasn't just some fleeting impulse. I wanted her to feel how deeply, how irrevocably, I was hers.

Her tongue teased mine as her fingers traced patterns on my skin, each touch electric. My hands roamed over her back, her sides, relearning every curve, every dip.

She made a soft sound of pleasure, and I felt a fierce satisfaction, a thrill that went all the way down to my bones. *This* was what I'd wanted. *She* was what I'd wanted—all of her. Her laughter, her strength, her vulnerability. Everything that made her Faye.

"You're sure?" I asked one more time, needing her to be certain.

She pulled back just enough to meet my eyes, her lips swollen from our kisses. "I've never been surer of anything."

I traced the curve of her cheek, memorizing the feel of her skin beneath my fingertips, etching every detail into my mind, because I knew I'd hold on to this moment forever. "Good. Because I've wanted this—wanted you—for so long."

Forever.

"Show me."

I pulled her close again, kissing her deeply, thoroughly, the way I'd dreamed of for years. Her hands slipped under my shirt, trailing fire across my skin as I explored her soft curves memorizing each new discovery.

If I only had this moment for the rest of my life, it would be enough.

"Sam," she breathed against my lips. "Take me to bed."

I groaned against her lips. "We live in a fucking bus."

"Then get a hotel room."

"Fuck."

I hit the intercom, calling the driver.

"Yes?" he asked.

"Find a hotel. Four Seasons, or the Sapphire."

"Yes, sir."

I turn back to Faye. "We'll never hear the end of this."

She grinned, her beauty stealing my breath.

"Shut up and kiss me."

9

FAYE

CURRENT STATUS REPORT

FREAKING OUT
Final Note: Oh God!!!

~

The Four Seasons lobby gleamed with understated elegance, all marble floors and soft lighting. I barely noticed any of it, too aware of the hand Sam had slipped under my coat to press against my lower back, the heat of his touch burning through my dress.

"Wait here," he murmured against my ear, his voice pitched low enough to make me shiver.

I watched him stride to the reception desk, all quiet confidence in his leather jacket and messy hair. A strand had fallen across his forehead—the same strand I'd run my fingers through just minutes ago in the car.

My lips still tingled from his kisses.

Focus, Faye.

But focusing was impossible when Sam kept glancing back at me, his dark eyes holding promises that made my knees weak. He was talking to the receptionist, his posture relaxed but I could see the tension in his shoulders, the way his fingers drummed against the counter.

He was nervous too.

Somehow that made everything better. Easier.

"All set." He appeared at my side, key cards in hand. His thumb brushed my wrist, a seemingly casual touch that sent electricity racing up my arm. "Ready?"

I caught his hand, threading our fingers together. "Yes."

His smile was soft, private—just for me. As we walked to the elevator, I realized this was really happening. After years of careful distance, of maintaining professional boundaries, of pretending I didn't notice how beautiful he was when he played...

The elevator doors closed, leaving us alone.

Sam's hand tightened on mine. "Having second thoughts?"

I turned to face him, taking in the uncertainty in his eyes. Even now, he was giving me an out.

"No." I stepped closer, smoothing my free hand over his chest. "But if you keep asking, I might think you are."

He caught my hand, pressing a kiss to my palm. "Never."

I leaned in to kiss him, but he stopped me with hands on my waist.

"If we start now, I won't stop."

I liked the possessive, almost feral roughness in his voice.

The elevator dinged, doors opening onto our floor. Sam guided me down the hallway, his thumb tracing patterns on my skin that made it hard to walk straight.

At our door, he paused. "Faye—"

I pulled him down by his shirt, kissing him before he could second-guess this—second-guess us. He groaned, pressing me against the door as he kissed me back, deep and thorough.

"Inside," I managed between kisses. "Now."

He fumbled with the key card, cursing softly as it took three tries to open the door. Then we were stumbling inside, hands everywhere, kisses growing desperate.

"Wait." He pulled back, breathing heavily. "We should... slow down."

"Why?"

"Because." He pressed his forehead to mine. "I want to savor. I want to memori—"

I caught his face between my hands, making him look at me. "Sam. I want you. All of you. We've wasted enough time being careful."

His eyes darkened. "Say that again."

"I want you."

With a growl, he pulled me close, capturing my mouth in a kiss that melted my bones. As his hands slid under my dress, I decided maybe lists weren't so bad after all.

"We'll go slow next time," he promised, nipping at my bottom lip.

His fingers traced patterns on my skin, leaving trails of fire in their wake. I arched into his touch, craving more. He obliged, his hands roaming higher until they cupped my breasts through the thin fabric. I moaned into the kiss, my own hands gripping his muscular back.

He walked us backwards until my legs hit the edge of the bed. With a gentle push, I fell back onto the soft mattress. He loomed over me, eyes dark with desire.

"You're so beautiful," he murmured, his gaze raking over my body appreciatively.

I reached up and pulled him down to me, needing to feel his weight pressing me into the sheets. Our kisses turned frantic, tongues tangling and teeth clashing. I tugged impatiently at his shirt, and he broke away just long enough to yank it over his head.

My hands mapped the planes of his chest, revealing in the feel of his warm skin and hard muscles. He groaned as I dragged my nails down his abs. His own hands were busy pushing my dress up around my waist.

"Off," he commanded gruffly, and I eagerly complied, wiggling out of the garment and tossing it aside. Now clad in only my bra and underwear, I watched as his eyes hungrily took me in.

I gasped as his hands found the seam of my panties, teasing me through the delicate fabric.

"Please," I breathed, arching into his touch. "I need you."

With a wicked grin, he dropped to his knees. He pressed a kiss to my inner thigh, his stubble grazing my sensitive skin. Slowly, torturously, he dragged my underwear down my legs, his eyes never leaving mine.

I whimpered as the cool air hit my heated flesh, my need for him growing with every passing second. He ran a finger through my wet heat, and I nearly arched off the bed, such was my need.

"So wet for me already," he murmured appreciatively. "Let's see how many times I can make you come."

I tangled my fingers in his hair, holding him in place as he licked and sucked, working me into a frenzy. He teased, alternating between rough and gentle, between hot, wet licks and blunt fingers. I became madness, writhing beneath him, pleading for release, losing all control as he drove me closer and closer to the edge.

"That's it, Faye," he growled between long, slow licks. "Let me hear you."

I let out a keening moan as he slid two fingers inside me, stroking in time with the swirls of his tongue. I fisted the sheets, incoherent pleas spilling from my lips.

He built me up slowly, bringing me to the edge again and again before easing off, keeping me suspended in sweet, aching bliss. When he finally let me fall, I shattered with a hoarse scream, my body shaking with the force of my release.

He growled his appreciation, holding me in place as he renewed his efforts, continuing his sensual assault until a second orgasm crashed over me.

Overwrought and oversensitive, I had to push weakly at his shoulders.

"Sam, too much," I gasped, my body languid and loose, trembling from the aftershocks.

He relented without protest, crawling up the bed, trailing kisses along my heated skin.

When his mouth met mine, I could taste myself on his tongue. It was erotic and intimate, and a new wave of desire washed over me.

"Your turn," I murmured, sliding a hand between our bodies to his fly. Slowly, I popped the buttons of his jeans. He hissed as I slid my hand inside, cupping him through his boxers.

He was hard and straining against the fabric, and I traced the outline of his impressive length, enjoying the way his breath hitched.

"Fuck."

I grinned, wrapping my fingers around his thick shaft, stroking him base to tip. He dropped his forehead to my shoulder with a low groan. Emboldened, I tightened my grip, twisting my wrist on the upstroke just the way I'd always imagined he'd like.

"Fuck, Faye," he panted against my skin. "You keep that up and this will be over before it starts."

I smiled, pleased at the effect I was having on him. "We can't have that."

I flipped us over so I was straddling his hips. His hands landed on my waist, gripping me tightly as I positioned myself over him.

"Wait." I froze. "Condom?"

He pointed at his wallet on the bedside table. "I might have one."

Grinning, I leaned across him only to be detoured when his mouth found my breast.

"Sam!" I gasped as his teeth grazed my nipple through the thin lace of my bra.

He hummed in response, the vibrations making me arch into his touch. His fingers deftly unhooked the clasp, freeing my breasts to his hungry gaze.

"So perfect," he murmured before capturing one tight peak between his lips.

I lost myself in the sensation, my head falling back as he lavished attention on my sensitive flesh. He alternated between soft licks and gentle nips, his hands roaming my body, setting me ablaze.

It took monumental effort, but I managed to pull away, ignoring his groan of protest. I found the condom and tore it open with my teeth. His eyes darkened as he watched me roll it onto his thick length.

Our eyes locked as I slowly sank down, taking him inch by delicious inch.

"Faye."

I loved the way he said my name, like a prayer, a praise, a wish. I started to move, rolling my hips in a steady rhythm. His hands guided me, urging me faster, deeper. I braced myself on his chest, my nails digging in. The only sounds were our ragged breaths and the obscene, delicious slap of skin on skin.

"Fuck, Faye," he growled, his fingers digging into my flesh. "You feel amazing."

I could only whimper in response, too lost in sensation to form coherent words. He felt incredible inside me, every drag of his hard length against my inner walls pushed me closer to the edge. Sensing my impending orgasm, he slid a hand between us, his thumb finding my clit.

"Come for me."

I cried out at the added stimulation, my movements becoming erratic as I chased my release, losing myself in the way he felt, he touched, he teased.

"Sam!"

"That's it, baby," he encouraged through clenched teeth. "Take it. Take me. Take everything."

My body trembled as waves of pleasure

crashed over me, my inner muscles clenching around him as I came undone. Sam groaned, his hips snapping forward to bury himself deep inside me as he found his own release.

For several long moments, we stayed locked together, hearts racing and chests heaving as we caught our breaths. Slowly, Sam lifted his head from where it rested against my neck, his dark eyes meeting mine. A satisfied smile curved his sensual lips.

"You're incredible," he murmured, brushing a tender kiss across my mouth. "I can never get enough of you."

I returned his smile, my fingers playing with the damp hair at the nape of his neck. "You're not so bad yourself."

He got rid of the condom and returned to the bed, pulling me against his side.

I nestled into him, my head pillowed on his broad chest, listening to the steady thump of his heartbeat. His fingers traced idle patterns along my spine as a sated silence enveloped us.

"Should this feel weird?" I asked softly.

"Maybe. Does it?"

I shook my head.

"Good." He tapped a finger against my temple. "Don't overthink this, Faye. It is what is it."

I tilted my head back. "And what is this, exactly?"

"The start of something great."

Chuckling, I snuggled closer into his side. "Okay. We should sleep though. You have a studio day tomorrow and interviews before the concert."

"Mm." He pressed a kiss to my head. "I'll wake you up early for round two."

"Can't wait."

10

FAYE

CURRENT STATUS REPORT

Basking in the afterglow
Notes: No notes. 10/10

～

Morning sunlight filtered through the hotel curtains, casting a warm glow across the room. I stretched lazily, my eyes adjusting to find Sam at the small desk by the window, bent over his notebook. His hair was still mussed from sleep and—if I'm honest—round number three.

Grinning, I rolled onto my side, tucking my hands under my cheek as I watched him. There was something about seeing him there, completely absorbed in his writing, that made my heart flutter.

"Early bird," I mumbled.

He startled slightly, laughing at his own surprise. "Morning, sleepyhead. How are you feeling today?"

I stretched, allowing the sheet to slip down and hover just over my nipples. "Well. You?"

His gaze locked on my breasts. "Never better."

"Do we have time for—" I groaned as my phone let out a cheery buzz. "Hold that thought. I need to take this."

He closed his notebook, setting it on the dresser. "I'll grab a shower, then go rustle us up some breakfast. Room service is gonna take too long."

"Sounds great."

I watched him walk toward the bathroom, his butt gloriously clad in his boxers as I answered. "Faye Moyo speaking."

"Ms. Moyo, this is David Cohen from *Rolling Stone*..."

My heart leapt. *Rolling Stone* had been our white whale since the band's second album.

"Mr. Cohen, hi, hello!" I scrambled, reaching for Sam's shirt as I juggled the phone.

"Call me Dave. Look, I know this is late notice but I've had a cancellation. Any chance you might be free on Wednesday to discuss that feature?"

"For you? Absolutely! Just tell me where and when."

"Great, let me give you the address."

"Sure, um... just let me..." I scrambled for something to write with as he discussed potential interview dates. The only thing within reach was Sam's notebook on the dresser.

"Just one moment," I said smoothly, flipping it open to a blank page at the back. But the page wasn't blank. My name caught my eye, stopping me cold.

FAYE COLOR-CODES EVERYTHING. EVEN HER PAPER CLIPS HAVE A SYSTEM. I SHOULDN'T FIND IT ADORABLE, BUT I DO.

"Faye?"

"I'm so sorry." I swallowed hard. "Could you email those dates? Something just came up that requires my immediate attention."

I managed to end the call professionally, but my hands were shaking as I lifted Sam's notebook.

SEPTEMBER 15
FAYE COLOR-CODES EVERYTHING. EVEN

HER PAPER CLIPS HAVE A SYSTEM. I
SHOULDN'T FIND IT ADORABLE, BUT I DO.
TODAY SHE ORGANIZED OUR ENTIRE
TOUR SCHEDULE WITH STICKY NOTES AND
MILITARY PRECISION. JUSTICE ACTUALLY
TOOK   NOTES.   SHE'S   KIND   OF
MAGNIFICENT WHEN SHE'S IN CONTROL.
ACTUALLY, SHE'S KIND OF MAGNIFICENT
ALL THE TIME.

I sank onto the bed, my heart
thundering.

The next page held lyrics, scratched out and
rewritten.

"SHE'S GOT EVERYTHING UNDER CONTROL.
EVERY MINUTE, EVERY MOMENT
BUT HONEY, IF YOU COULD SEE
HOW BEAUTIFUL YOU ARE WHEN YOU
LET GO
WHEN YOU SMILE WITHOUT PLANNING
WHEN YOU LAUGH WITHOUT WARNING
WHEN YOU JUST LET YOURSELF BE..."

I recognized that song. It had been on their
second album, the one that earned them their
first platinum record. I'd always assumed it was

about some free-spirited girl who'd caught Sam's eye.

Not about... not about me.

My fingers trembled as I turned the page.

DECEMBER 3

SHE FELL ASLEEP AT HER DESK AGAIN. THIRD TIME THIS WEEK. I MOVED HER TO THE COUCH AND COVERED HER WITH MY JACKET. SHE CURLED INTO IT LIKE IT WAS MEANT FOR HER. MAYBE IT WAS. MAYBE EVERYTHING I HAVE HAS ALWAYS BEEN MEANT FOR HER.

NOTE: REMEMBER SHE LIKES HER COFFEE EXTRA HOT IN THE MORNING AFTER LATE NIGHTS. AND MAYBE BUY A BETTER BLANKET FOR THE OFFICE COUCH.

The next pages were filled with more lyrics, more notes. Small observations that I'd never noticed him making.

SHE TOUCHES HER LEFT EAR WHEN SHE'S NERVOUS IN INTERVIEWS.

HER LAUGH HAS DIFFERENT LEVELS – POLITE (CLIENTS), GENUINE (FRIENDS),

UNCONTROLLED (RARE BUT WORTH
WAITING FOR).
SHE STILL CARRIES THAT REJECTION
LETTER IN HER WALLET. I WISH I
COULD SHOW HER HOW AMAZING
SHE IS.

Then came the lyrics that broke me:

"EVERYONE SEES THE PERFECT SMILE
THE POLISHED SHINE, THE CAREFUL
STYLE
BUT I SEE THE STORMS YOU'RE HIDING
BEHIND THOSE BRIGHT BROWN EYES
LET ME BE YOUR SHELTER
LET ME BE YOUR SHADE
YOU DON'T HAVE TO WEATHER
EVERY STORM ALONE..."

I remembered the date he wrote that. It was
the day Alex had stolen my campaign and
destroyed my career. I'd been trying so hard to
hold it together, to prove I was professional
despite the betrayal. Sam had simply appeared
with coffee and sat with me in silence until I
could breathe again.

I'd never known he'd gone home and written about it.

More pages. More songs. More pieces of me seen through his eyes.

Just a brown-eyed boy in love with a brown-eyed girl—written the night of our first major awards show.

The girl with the lists—after I'd organized their first international press tour.

Control Freak—which wasn't mocking like I'd always assumed, but tender, understanding.

Years of love, hidden in plain sight.

Years of him seeing me, supporting me, loving me... and never asking for anything in return.

A drop of water hit the page. I touched my cheek, surprised to find tears.

The door clicked behind me.

"So do you want a bagel or—shit. Faye?"

And suddenly it was too much. Too real. Too...

I stood, clutching his notebook like a lifeline. Our gazes met, his startled, vulnerable, raw.

"When?"

He didn't have to ask what I meant.

"Forever."

I closed my eyes, absorbing his confession. Fuck. This wasn't a fleeting crush for him, wasn't some impulsive spark he'd only recently felt. This was something he'd been carrying for years, something he'd woven into the very fabric of our lives. *Forever.* The word echoed through me, terrifying in its certainty.

Because Sam loving me like this didn't just change things—it upended everything. All my carefully constructed walls, the years I'd spent building a career, crafting my image, keeping my heart under lock and key. My control was my armor, my way of keeping everything neat, planned, predictable. I'd told myself that if I kept things organized, if I always stayed one step ahead, I'd be safe. I wouldn't get hurt. No one could touch me.

But Sam... Sam had somehow slipped past those defenses, quietly, without asking. He'd seen through my walls, my systems, my need for control. He'd seen *me.*

Terror ripped through me, fear cold and brutal. I had no color-coded system for this. No carefully planned strategy. No control.

I pressed my hand to my mouth, trying to contain the sob building in my throat. My carefully constructed walls, all my perfect plans, all my need for control... none of it seemed to matter anymore.

Because Sam had written our story in the margins of this notebook.

And I hadn't even known I was the main character.

My phone buzzed, another incoming call.

"I need to take this." I turned away.

"Faye, don't. Let's—"

"I need you to leave."

I heard Sam stop behind me.

"Faye."

"Please," I whispered, barely holding myself together. "Just give me some time."

I heard him moving around, before the door opened.

"I'm sorry I hid the truth," he said softly. "But just know, I've never lied. Please, don't hate me."

I sighed, glancing at him over my shoulder. "I don't hate you. I just need time to... adjust."

He nodded. "Will you be at the concert tonight?"

I forced myself to nod, knowing he needed something, some sign that I wasn't pulling away entirely, even if that's exactly what I felt like doing. The thought of facing him tonight, of seeing him onstage, of knowing that every lyric, every look, every smile might be meant for me —it scared me. But I couldn't bring myself to say no.

His shoulders relaxed slightly, as if that one promise was enough for now. "Okay."

With that, he slipped out the door, leaving me alone with the buzzing phone, the quiet hotel room, and the notebook still open in my hands. As the door clicked shut, the weight of it all settled over me—years of friendship, hidden feelings, a love I hadn't known existed, all crashing down like a wave—threatening to pull me under.

My hands shook as I closed the notebook, feeling the walls I'd so carefully built beginning to crack, leaving me exposed, uncertain, vulnerable. And for the first time in my life, I had no plan, no strategy, no way to keep myself safe from the storm Sam had unleashed in me.

11

SAM

- Wild Ones, "The Girl"

~

I closed the door behind me, hating myself for leaving her alone in there, knowing exactly how her mind worked, how she'd twist and turn over every word she'd read, every lyric, every note. She'd be overthinking it, dissecting the years of feelings I'd tried to keep hidden, wondering how she could have missed it, doubting every moment. Part of me wanted to barge back in, to grab her and make her understand that none of this changed anything—except that now she knew.

But maybe that was what scared her most. And, if I were honest, it scared me too.

I took a deep breath, trying to steady myself, but I couldn't shake the strange mix of emotions twisting in my chest. For years, I'd been careful, methodical, hiding how I felt, shoving it all into quiet moments and notebooks and songs I'd thought she'd never know were about her. It was safer that way; it was easier to keep her as my friend, my partner, and tell myself that was enough.

And yet... a part of me was *relieved.* Relieved she'd found the notebook, relieved that, finally, she'd seen it all. I'd always worried about what would happen if she knew, if she saw how deep my feelings ran, if she understood how much of my life—hell, how much of *me*—was wrapped up in her. I'd thought it would be terrifying, like standing in front of a firing squad, but now, walking down the quiet hall, I realized I felt lighter.

She knew.

She'd seen all of it, every line and lyric and late-night confession I'd scribbled in the margins. She'd seen my heart laid bare, and even if it had shaken her, she hadn't run.

She'd even said she'd be there tonight.

And that—that tiny glimmer of hop—was enough to keep me moving, to keep me from turning back around and barging into that hotel room to try and explain what I could barely put into words. It was the hope that maybe, just maybe, we could move forward. Together. Or at least... that I could finally let myself hope.

I made my way—shirtless I might add—back to the arena. The bus was quiet, the band out somewhere.

My phone buzzed and I practically fumbled it as I pulled it from my pocket.

FAYEMOYO

One question – when we were together, were you only ever imagining this? Us being in a relationship?

My fingers hovered over the screen as I considered how to respond.

SAMDOGG

No. But only because I never let myself imagine the possibility of us.

I watched the three little dots appear and

disappear, then reappear and disappear once more.

FAYEMOYO

Never?

My answer was simple and honest.

SAMDOGG

What we had before was always more than enough.

FAYEMOYO

I'm not sure if that's the correct answer or super depressing, but thank you for not being a creep. At least not today.

The tension that had twisted around my heart relaxed a fraction, allowing me to draw breath for the first time since I'd left her in the hotel room.

It wasn't forgiveness, but it was a start.

Without thinking, I picked up my guitar, absently strumming as a whisper of a lyric took root.

The thing about being a songwriter is that sometimes the music says what you can't.

I let my fingers find chords that matched the ache in my chest. The melody that emerged was soft, tentative—like the way Faye had touched the notebook before shit hit the fan.

My phone buzzed with an incoming text.

JUSTICE

Get your ass down to the arena

SAMDOGG

No

JUSTICE

Not a request, brother. Band
meeting. Now.

I sighed, setting down my guitar. The last thing I wanted was company, but five years of being in a band had taught me that ignoring a "band meeting" only led to them bringing the meeting to you.

Usually with alcohol.

Always with opinions.

The backstage of the arena was quiet this early in the morning, just a few roadies and crew checking different things ahead of our gig later today.

I found them in the greenroom, our regular security detail by the door.

Justice, Felix, and Radley were bent over a table, their heads practically touching like they were plotting something.

They probably were.

"There he is!" Justice called out. "Our resident lover boy."

"Don't," I warned, sliding into the spare chair.

"What? I'm just saying, if I'd known you were going to not come home last night I wouldn't have waited up."

I snorted. "As fucking if." I glanced around the table. "What's this about?"

"Call it a romance intervention." Justice leaned forward. "Is she in love with you yet?"

A knife cut through my chest, piercing my heart.

"Justice." Radley's tone held a warning.

"Fine." He pushed a glass toward me. "Drink. You look like you need it."

I took the drink but didn't sip it. "Why am I here?"

"Because," Felix said, "you're an idiot."

"Thanks."

"A well-meaning idiot," Radley added kindly. "But still an idiot."

I rubbed a hand over my face. "If this is an intervention—"

"This is us," Justice cut in, suddenly serious, "telling you to stop hiding."

"I'm not—"

"Dude." Felix leaned forward. "You've been in love with Faye since before we were even a band. You wrote an entire album's worth of songs about her. You married her—drunk or not, that wasn't an accident."

"And now," Radley continued, "when you have the chance to do something romantic and declare you're love, you're piss-farting around with your dick in your hand. You need to be fighting for her."

I rolled my tongue over my teeth. "She knows."

That took the wind out of their sails.

"What?"

"And she said she needed time."

"And you're giving it to her because that's what you do." Justice's voice was gentler now. "You give and give and never ask for anything back. But, brother, sometimes you have to fight for what you want."

"I don't want to pressure her."

"It's not pressure to be honest." Radley reached across the table, squeezing my hand. "She deserves to know everything. Not just the songs, but why you wrote them. Why you kept them hidden. Why you've stayed silent all these years."

I stared into my untouched drink. "She'll overthink this. Try to work out why we don't make sense."

"Maybe." Justice shrugged. "Or maybe she'll come around. Who the fuck knows?"

"Not me," I muttered.

"Oh for—" Radley threw her hands up. "Are you actually blind? Have you not seen how she looks at you? How she takes care of you? How she's the only one you let close enough to really see you?"

"That's just Faye. She takes care of everyone."

"No." Felix's voice was firm. "She takes care of the band because it's her job. She takes care of you because she wants to."

"There's a difference between professional Faye who manages our careers," Justice added. "And your Faye who knows exactly how you take your coffee and carries pain relievers for your shoulder. She watches you during every performance like you're the only person in the room."

I opened my mouth to argue, then closed it as memories hit me.

Faye adjusting my guitar strap before I even noticed it was twisted.

Her hand on my back when crowds got too overwhelming.

The way she'd started wearing my favorite perfume after I'd mentioned once that it reminded me of home.

"Oh," I breathed. "I never..."

"Finally," Justice muttered. "He gets it."

"But she ran."

"Because Faye needs to process." Radley's smile was knowing. "She likes to understand things, to categorize them. And you just handed her years she has to recontextualize. Give her time but not too much."

"And continue fighting for her," Felix added. "Women love that shit."

We all looked at him.

"And how, exactly, would you know that?" Radley asked, arching her eyebrow.

"I read romance."

Justice threw a pen at him.

"So what are you proposing?" I asked, glancing around the table. "I can tell you already have plans cooking."

Justice's grin turned wicked. "Funny you should say that..."

"Why am I suddenly terrified?"

"Because you're smart." Radley laughed. "But trust us. We've got your back."

"Always have," Felix added.

I looked at my family—this weird, wonderful group of people who'd seen my love for Faye long before I'd admitted it to myself.

"Love you guys," I said gruffly. "Now, what's the plan?"

Justice's grin widened. "How do you feel about performing a solo at tonight's show?"

My heart stopped. "Fuck. That's…" I swallowed hard. "That's terrifying."

"Good." Radley squeezed my hand again. "Time to lay it all on the line, lover boy."

I thought about Faye reading my notebook. About years of loving her in silence. About how tired I was of pretending this fake marriage wasn't everything I'd ever wanted.

"Okay." I picked up my drink, finally taking a sip of the cool soda. "Let's do it."

Because maybe what we had wasn't enough anymore.

Not for either of us.

12

FAYE

EMOTIONAL CRISIS MANAGEMENT
PLAN

Priority Level: CATASTROPHIC
Status: COMPLETE MELTDOWN

CURRENT SITUATION:
☐ In possession of Sam's song
notebook
☐ Emotions: Unregulated

IMMEDIATE CONCERNS:
1. Unable to create spreadsheet
for feelings
2. Sam's lyrics keep making me cry
3. Running out of sticky notes
Note: STOP CRYING ON THE NOTEBOOK

EMERGENCY ACTIONS REQUIRED:
A) Make PowerPoint presentation
[Pros and Cons]
B) Create comprehensive data
analysis
C) Color-code everything
D) STOP READING SAMS JOURNAL
(FAILING)

Current Status: T-minus 8 hours to
showtime
Threat Level: BEYOND CRITICAL

Personal Note: What if I've loved
him all along?

Secondary Note: Need more colored
tabs

Final Note: This was never
pretend, was it?

~

I ended up at Trent and Ryan's at midday, clutching Sam's notebook and trying not to fall apart.

"I can't control it," I blurted when Trent

opened the door. "I can't... I can't make a plan for this."

My brother took one look at me and pulled me into a hug. "Come on, sis. I'll make tea."

Their house was quiet, warm winter light softly shining through the glass windows. Photos of their life together lined the walls—Trent and Ryan's wedding, Seth's and Emma's adoption days, family gatherings—all showing love didn't have to be perfect to be real.

Decorations from Christmas and Thanksgiving still peeked out here and there—a pumpkin now covered in tinsel, a row of multicolored fairy lights, a discarded elf on a shelf.

Their home had love and life in it. And I loved that for my brother.

"The kids are at Mom and Dad's for the weekend," Trent explained, guiding me to their kitchen. "And Ryan's working late on a case."

I sank into a chair at their breakfast bar, still clutching Sam's notebook. "I'm sorry for just showing up."

"Please." He started the kettle. "Like you haven't sat through plenty of my crises."

"That's different. You always knew what you wanted." I traced the worn edge of Sam's notebook. "You knew you loved Ryan, even when you were apart."

"Ah." He leaned against the counter. "So this is about Sam."

"Did everyone know?" The words came out sharper than intended. "Was I the only one who didn't see it?"

"To be fair, you were a bit busy trying to control everything else."

"I don't—" I caught his knowing look. "Fine. Maybe I do. But that's my job. To manage things. To keep everything running smoothly."

"And how's that working out for your heart?"

I dropped my head to the counter with a groan. "When did you get so annoyingly insightful?"

"Probably around the time I stopped trying to control everything and admitted I was in love with my best friend." He set a mug of tea in front of me. "Sound familiar?"

"It's not the same."

"No?" He pulled out the chair beside me. "Let's see... years of friendship, fear of ruining what you have, one person quietly pining while the other remains oblivious..."

"You then broke up. For years."

"I was a fool." He waggled a finger at me. "Which means you should learn from my mistakes."

"I hate you."

"You love me." He nudged my shoulder. "Just like you love Sam."

The word made my chest tight. "I can't."

"Why not? You married him."

I flushed, turning away. "That might have been a drunken mistake."

"No kidding? The unicorn celebrant certainly didn't tip me off." He rolled his eyes. "Go on, tell me why it's impossible to have fallen in love with a guy who acts like you hung the moon."

"Because..." I sat up, wrapping my hands around the warm mug. "Because if I admit that, if I let myself feel that, then everything changes. The band dynamic, our professional relationship, everything we've built... it all becomes complicated."

"News flash, sis. You're already married to him."

"That's different. That's..." I waved a hand. "Manageable. This is..."

"Real?"

"Terrifying."

Trent was quiet for a moment, studying me. "You know what scared me most about loving Ryan?"

"What?"

"That I couldn't control his response. I could plan the perfect moment, say the perfect words, but in the end, I couldn't control whether he loved me back." He smiled softly. "Turns out, I didn't need to. The messy, unplanned reality was better than anything I could have orchestrated."

"But what if it goes wrong?" My voice cracked. "What if I lose him completely?"

"What if you don't?" He gestured to the notebook. "From what I can see, that boy's been loving you steadily for years. Through crazy schedules and professional crises and everything else. Maybe it's time to stop managing and start feeling."

"I don't know how."

"Yes, you do." He squeezed my hand. "You just have to be brave enough to try."

I took a sip of my mug, mulling over his words.

I loved Sam. There wasn't any doubt of that. But what really concerned me, what threw up the barrier between me loving and me wanting to be loved was exactly what Trent had identified.

Fear.

I feared Sam hurting me like Alex had. I feared not having control of my emotions, my life, my decisions. I feared he'd break my heart.

But every piece of evidence I had about Sam pointed to the opposite.

Damn.

"Trent?" I gripped my mug tighter. "I need your laptop."

"Why do I feel like I'm about to witness peak Faye organization?"

"Because you are." I pulled out my phone, already creating a new folder. "I need to make a PowerPoint."

His laugh was warm and knowing. "Of course you do."

"Don't mock me. This is important. This is..." I gestured at the notebook. "He gave me songs. Beautiful, heartfelt songs. I need to give him something that's... that's me."

"And that's a PowerPoint presentation?"

"No." I straightened in my chair. "It's a comprehensive five-year plan, complete with contingencies, projected outcomes, and risk assessments, presented in my signature color-coded style with appropriate graphs and—why are you looking at me like that?"

Trent's smile was soft. "Because this might be the most perfectly *you* way to say 'I love you' that I've ever heard."

"You think it's too much."

"I think Sam's going to love it precisely because it's too much." He stood to retrieve his laptop. "It's you being unapologetically you.

Planning and organizing your way through feelings instead of running from them."

I opened the laptop, fingers flying over the keys. "I'm going to need sticky notes. And that fancy paper you use for your fire department presentations. And—"

"The color-coded tabs from your emergency PR kit you keep at Mom and Dad's?"

"Yes! And—"

"Your backup external hard drive with all the band's photos from the last five years?"

"How did you—"

"Because I know you." He was already reaching for his keys. "And I know you've documented every moment without realizing you were creating a love story. Want me to grab it while you start your slides?"

I launched PowerPoint, already formatting my title slide. "Yes. And Trent?"

"Yeah?"

"Can you call Liz? I need statistics on successful marriages that started as friendships. And maybe some data on music industry relationship longevity. For the analytics section."

"The ana—you know what? Never mind. Of course you need an analytics section." He kissed the top of my head. "I'll call her. Anything else?"

I looked at my growing outline:

- Slide 1: Executive Summary
  - Why Sam Dogg Should
  Consider a Permanent
  Merger of Hearts
- Slide 2: Historical
  Context - A Five-Year
  Analysis of Unconscious
  Love
- Slide 3: Risk Assessment -
  Why I Ran (And Why I'm
  Done Running)
- Slide 4: Market Analysis -
  Why We Work Better
  Together
- Slide 5: Future
  Projections - Vision Board
  for Years 1-5, 5-10, 10-50
- Slide 6-39: Detailed
  Supporting Evidence
- Slide 40: Proposed Next
  Steps

"Yes," I said. "I need every photo you have of Sam with the kids. Especially that one from Seth's birthday when Sam taught him to play 'Yellow Submarine.'"

"For the presentation?"

"For the 'Why You're an Amazing Uncle' section. It's going in right after the real estate market analysis for potential future homes."

Trent's laugh echoed down the hall. "Only you would include a real estate analysis in a love declaration."

"It's called being thorough!"

"It's called being Faye," he called back. "And that's exactly why it's perfect."

I turned back to the laptop, heart racing but hands steady as I began to type.

```
Presentation Objective
To provide comprehensive evidence
supporting the transition from
temporary marriage arrangement to
permanent partnership, with
detailed analysis of past
indicators, present compatibility
metrics, and future growth
potential.


Key Deliverable
One (1) happily ever after,
metrics to be determined by mutual
agreement of involved parties.
```

Because maybe this was how I loved—with plans and spreadsheets and color-coded tabs.

Maybe this was my love song.

13

SAME

~

Every song I've ever sung
Has been a love letter in
disguise
Tonight I'm done with hiding
Some write their love in verses
Some paint it in the stars
But baby, my love was written
In color-coded charts

- The Wild Ones, "Love by
Numbers"

The thing about performing is that sometimes the lights are so bright you can't see the audience.

Sometimes that's a curse.

Tonight, it was a blessing.

"You ready for this?" Justice asked as we waited in the wings. The roar of the crowd vibrated through my bones, but for once, my racing heart had nothing to do with stage fright.

"No." I adjusted my guitar strap. "But I'm doing it anyway."

"That's my boy." He clapped my shoulder. "For what it's worth, I haven't seen Faye all day."

My stomach twisted. "Thanks. That's... not super helpful."

He grinned. "She'll be here. I know it."

"Places!" the stage manager called out.

This was it. No turning back.

We took our positions on the darkened stage—Justice center, me to his right, Felix and Radley creating our foundation. The same setup we'd had for years, except nothing felt the same.

Because tonight, I wasn't just Sam Dogg, lead guitarist of The Wild Ones.

Tonight, I was just a boy with a guitar, finally brave enough to tell the truth.

The lights hit. The crowd roared. And we played.

Song after song, building the energy, feeding off the audience's response. I played on autopilot, my mind already on the final number. On the words I'd written in margins and hotel rooms and quiet moments watching Faye work.

Finally, Justice stepped up to his mic. "You've been amazing tonight!"

The crowd roared their approval.

"But we've got one more song for you. Something new. Something..." His eyes found mine. "Something real."

My heart thundered as I stepped up to my own mic. This wasn't unusual—we often shared vocals.

"This one's called 'Maybe That's Enough,'" I said quietly. "And it's for the girl who's been running my world since high school."

I glanced at the wing hoping Faye would be there, only to see her spot empty.

Fuck.

The opening chords felt different under stadium lights. More exposed. More real.

Fuck. Here we go.

"Early morning coffee runs
Late night sound checks
You've got the world on your shoulders
And I've got you on my mind
The way you scrunch your nose at my jokes

How you know just when I need
A gentle word, a quiet moment
Maybe that's enough."

I closed my eyes, letting the melody carry me. Letting years of quiet love pour into every note.

"Maybe it's enough to love you from the wings
While you orchestrate everything
Maybe it's enough to catch you when you fall
Though you never fall at all
Maybe it's enough to know your perfect pace
To match your steps in this dance we face
Maybe loving you in silence
Maybe that's enough."

Justice's harmony wrapped around the chorus, supporting but never overshadowing. Radley and Felix joined in, adding to and building the song. The crowd swayed, phone lights creating a sea of stars.

But I wasn't singing for them. I was singing for the woman who had my heart wrapped in her fist.

"You count breaths between disasters
I count moments till you smile
You're arranging all our chaos

Into neat and perfect rows
And I'm collecting all these seconds
Like photographs I'll never show
Of how you look when you're unguarded
When your walls are running low."

We shifted into the chorus, and I forced my eyes open, watching the sea of light dance before me in the cold winter air.

"Maybe it's enough to love you from the wings
While you orchestrate everything
Maybe it's enough to catch you when you fall
Though you never fall at all
Maybe it's enough to know your perfect pace
To match your steps in this dance we face
Maybe loving you in silence
Maybe that's enough."

My voice wavered on the last line. I turned, ready to launch into the final chorus, and that's when I saw her.

Faye.

Standing in the wings where she always stood, but different. Her eyes were bright, her cheeks flushed, and in her hands... was that a laptop?

I turned directly toward her, singing to her,

pouring myself into each word, each note, each
breath.

"But what if it's not enough?
What if I'm tired of pretending?
What if every song I've written
Has been begging you to see
That maybe we could be

Everything we're just pretending.

Maybe it's not enough to watch you anymore
Maybe we could be something more
Maybe it's time to step out of the wings
And show you everything
Maybe loving you in silence
Was never enough at all
Maybe we could be something more
Maybe that'll be enough.

But what if it's not enough?
What if I'm tired of pretending?
What if every song I've written
Has been begging you to see
That maybe we could be

Everything we're just pretending.

Maybe it's not enough to watch you anymore

Maybe we could be something more
Maybe that'll be enough."

The final note faded. The crowd erupted.

And I couldn't look away from Faye.

She didn't run.

She didn't hide.

She just stood there, watching me with a look I'd never seen before—a mix of nerves and something softer, something vulnerable.

That's when I knew she'd been listening to every word, that she'd heard the confession woven through every line, every chord. My heart pounded as I took her in, every detail crystal clear against the darkened backdrop of the crowd.

There was something new in her eyes, something raw and unguarded, and it took me a moment to realize that she was looking at me like she *saw* me—really saw me. Her look sent a jolt of electricity through me, made my breath catch in a way I wasn't prepared for. I'd laid myself bare tonight, letting her hear every hidden piece of my heart, and now... now, she was looking at me like she understood.

Like maybe she felt it too.

She held out her hand, a smile I'd never seen before—part nerves, part determined, all Faye.

I handed my guitar to a waiting tech and crossed to her, heart in my throat.

"Faye, I—"

"Shut up." She grabbed my hand. "Come with me."

Confused and hurting, I did exactly as she asked.

14

FAYE

PRESENTATION EXECUTION PROTOCOL

Priority Level: LIFE-CHANGING
Status: TERRIFIED BUT DETERMINED

FINAL CHECKLIST:
☐ Laptop fully charged
☐ Backup drive secured
☐ ~~40 44 43 48 51~~ *52* slides
perfected
☐ Real estate analysis updated
☐ Breathing exercises completed
☐ Stop adding new slides!!!

POTENTIAL COMPLICATIONS:
1. Technical difficulties

2. Emotional overload
3. Sam's smile
4. Sam's eyes
5. Sam
Note: FOCUS ON PRESENTATION

CONTINGENCY PLANS:
A) Backup PowerPoint on phone
B) Hard copies of key slides
C) Emergency exit routes mapped
D) Cardiac resuscitation plan

KEY PRESENTATION POINTS:
- Statistical evidence of
compatibility
- Future projection models
- Risk/reward analysis
- The way he makes my heart race
Note: EMPHASIZE LAST ITEM

Current Status: T-minus 2 minutes
to revelation
Threat Level: MAXIMUM
Personal Note: Just tell him you
love him

~

The thing about controlling everything is that sometimes the most powerful moments come when you finally let go.

I'd watched Sam up there on that stage tonight and the whole world had faded into the background as he stepped into the spotlight, alone but for the guitar in his hands.

I'd seen the look in his eyes—focused, intense, like he was about to pour every part of himself into the song. And when he started to play, every chord, every lyric, I'd known it was written just for me.

I was in awe of his courage—how he'd stood there, putting everything on the line, without knowing if I'd feel the same way. He'd spent years quietly loving me, supporting me, waiting for the moment when I'd finally be ready to let him in. Tonight, even knowing he might lose me, he'd taken that leap, baring his heart in front of thousands of people, just to make sure I knew what I meant to him.

He made me realize just how afraid I'd been. How many years I'd spent building walls, creating a life that was so carefully curated, so meticulously planned, because deep down I was terrified of being vulnerable. I was terrified of letting someone see the real me, the messy parts, the parts that didn't have all the answers.

But Sam... he already knew. And he loved me in spite of it all. Despite of it all. Or maybe *because* of it all.

I pulled Sam into his trailer, my laptop clutched in my free hand, my heart thundering against my ribs. He looked beautiful and uncertain in the soft lighting, still wearing his stage clothes—dark jeans and a black button-down with the sleeves rolled up. His hair was damp with sweat, his eyes wide with something between hope and hurt.

"Faye—"

"No." I held up a hand. "You got to say everything with your songs. Now it's my turn."

I opened my laptop, hands shaking slightly as I pulled up my presentation. Fifty-two slides of my heart laid bare in the only way I knew how.

Sam's eyes widened as he saw the title slide.

A COMPREHENSIVE ANALYSIS OF WHY SAMUEL DOGG AND FAYE MOYO SHOULD CONSIDER A PERMANENT MERGER OF HEARTS: A FIVE TO FIFTY YEAR PROJECTION IN 50 SLIDES

A LAUGH BURST from his chest—surprised and tender and a little bit wet. "Of course."

"What?"

"Of course you'd answer my heart's song with spreadsheets and slides." His smile was soft, wondering. "Of course you'd plan your way into loving me."

"I..." My carefully prepared script fled. "Is that okay?"

He crossed to me in two strides, one hand cupping my face while the other steadied my laptop. "Faye Moyo, it's the most perfect thing I've ever seen."

"You haven't even seen the real estate analysis yet."

"There's a real estate analysis?"

"With projected market valuations for potential future homes." I bit my lip. "And a separate section on dog parks. And maybe a timeline for..." I gestured vaguely. "You know. Future occupants."

"Future..." His eyes widened. "Faye, did you make a PowerPoint about our future fur-babies?"

"I made a PowerPoint about everything." I set the laptop down, suddenly needing my hands free. "Because that's what I do. I plan. I organize. I control. But you..." I touched his chest, feeling his heart race under my palm. "You make me want to color outside the lines a little."

"Only a little?" His hand was warm on my cheek.

"Baby steps." I managed a shaky smile. "I did include a projected timeline for spontaneous date nights. Color-coded by activity level and required preparation time."

He laughed again, that full, rich sound I'd unknowingly been collecting for years. "I love you."

"I know. I have an entire section analyzing the linguistic patterns in your lyrics that—"

His kiss cut me off.

And for once in my life, I didn't mind losing control of the narrative.

When we finally parted, his forehead resting against mine, I whispered, "I love you too. In case that wasn't clear from the fifty-two slides of statistical evidence."

"Fifty-two? The presentation said fifty?"

"I may have added a few while waiting in the wings." I wound my arms around his neck. "The last two are about tonight's song and its impact on our relationship metrics."

"You're incredible." He kissed me again, softer this time. "Absolutely incredible."

"So... you want to see the rest of the presentation?"

His smile lit up his whole face. "Baby, I want

to see every color-coded chart you've ever made."

I reached for my laptop, but he caught my hand.

"But first..." He pulled me close again. "I think I need to kiss you some more. You know, for the data set."

"That's not very professional," I murmured against his lips.

"Good thing I'm not trying to be professional anymore." His eyes were bright with joy and mischief. "I'm just a brown-eyed boy in love with a brown-eyed girl who plans happiness in perfect little rows."

"And graphs," I added. "Don't forget the graphs."

"Never." He kissed my nose. "They're my favorite part."

And somehow, that was the most romantic thing he could have said.

His next kiss was different—deeper, hungrier. The kind of kiss that made PowerPoint presentations seem very far away. I pressed closer, feeling his heart race under my palm as his hands slid down my back.

"We should..." I gasped as his mouth found my neck. "The presentation..."

"Later." His voice was rough against my skin. "Right now I need..."

"What?"

He pulled back, his eyes dark and earnest. "You. Just you. No plans, no pretending. Just us."

Something inside me melted. "Sam..."

"Tell me to stop."

I wound my fingers in his hair, pulling him back to me. "Don't you dare."

His hands found the zipper of my dress as mine worked on his shirt buttons. Every touch felt charged, important. This wasn't like the desperate heat of the elevator. This was slower, sweeter, but somehow more intense.

Because this time we weren't pretending.

This time we weren't running.

This time we were choosing this. Choosing us.

"You're thinking too much," he murmured, pressing kisses along my collarbone.

"I'm always thinking too much."

His laugh vibrated against my skin. "I know. It's one of the things I love about you."

He backed me toward the small bed in the corner of his trailer, laying me down with a gentleness that made my heart ache.

"You're beautiful," he whispered, looking at me like I was something precious. "So damn beautiful."

I reached for him, needing him closer.

Needing to show him with touch what I couldn't say with words. His skin was warm under my hands, familiar from years of careful distance, new with permission to explore.

When he finally moved over me, his weight a perfect anchor, something settled in my chest. Like coming home. Like finding something I hadn't known I was missing.

"Faye?" His voice was soft, uncertain.

"Yes?"

"I've loved you for so long."

I pulled him down to me, letting my body say what my heart had been too scared to admit. I let myself get lost in the feel of him, in the sounds he made, in the way he whispered my name like a prayer.

For once, I didn't try to control anything.

Didn't try to plan.

Just felt.

Just loved.

Just... was.

After, when we lay tangled in sheets and moonlight, his fingers tracing patterns on my spine, I whispered, "I added a contingency plan for this, you know."

His laugh rumbled under my ear. "Of course you did."

"Slide forty-seven." I pressed a kiss to his

chest. "Physical compatibility metrics and projected intimacy schedules."

"Schedules?" He rolled us so he could look at me properly. "You made a sex schedule?"

"I like to be thorough."

His kiss was soft, laughing. "Show me."

"Now?"

"Mmm." His hands started wandering again. "We should probably make sure your data is accurate. For science."

I reached for my laptop. "I did include several scenarios that require immediate testing..."

"God, I love you." He pulled me back into his arms, catching my mouth in a hungry kiss.

Happy New Year to me.

EPILOGUE

FAYE

One Year Later

ANNIVERSARY PERFORMANCE CHECKLIST

Priority Level: PERFECT
Status: BLISSFULLY CHAOTIC

ONE YEAR ASSESSMENT:
- ☐ Red dress located
- ☐ Wedding ring polished
- ☐ Sam properly distracted
- ☐ Contingency plans updated
- ☐ Heart: Still racing (acceptable)

NOTABLE IMPROVEMENTS FROM LAST
YEAR:

1. Control: Strategically relaxed
2. Lists: Now include heart emojis
3. Sam: Officially permanent
4. Happiness: Off the charts
5. Love: Exponential growth
Note: DATA SUPPORTS ALL FINDINGS

CELEBRATION PROTOCOLS:
A) Kiss husband at midnight
B) Ignore Justice's commentary
C) Remember every moment
D) Make new memories

THINGS THAT HAVEN'T CHANGED:
- Sam's smile still melts me
- Still making lists
- Still planning everything
- Still madly in love
Note: SOME THINGS DON'T NEED
CHANGING

New Year's Resolution:
Nil.

Personal Note: Best impulsive decision ever

~

The thing about New Year's Eve is that sometimes the best moments come full circle.

"You're not seriously wearing that dress again," Sam said from the doorway of our bedroom, his eyes dark as he took in the red fabric.

"It's tradition." I smoothed down the fabric, fighting a smile as his gaze tracked the movement. "Besides, you like this dress."

"I like you in any thing." He crossed to me, wrapping his arms around my waist from behind. "Or nothing."

"We're going to be late."

"We're the main act." His lips found that spot behind my ear that still made my knees weak. "They can't start without us."

"Sam..."

"Five minutes?"

"That line didn't work last time either." But I leaned back into him anyway. "And we were an hour late to the studio."

"Worth it."

A knock at our door saved me from giving in to the look in his eyes.

"If you two are having sex again, I swear to God—" Justice's voice carried through the wood. "We have a show in forty minutes!"

"We're coming!" I called back, laughing as Sam muttered. "not yet," against my neck.

"Better not be!"

Sam's hands squeezed my hips once before releasing me. "One of these days I'm changing all the locks."

"No, you won't." I turned to straighten his bow tie. "You love them."

"I love you more."

"That's not in the data." But I kissed him anyway, quick and soft. "Come on. We have a show to do."

The energy in the venue was electric, reminiscent of that night a year ago when everything changed. The crowd seemed to pulse with anticipation as midnight approached.

One minute and thirteen seconds to go.

"Before we start the countdown," Sam's voice carried over the crowd as he stepped up to the mic. "I want to say something."

I paused in my usual spot in the wings, something warm unfurling in my chest as he found me with his eyes.

"A year ago tonight, I married the love of my life." The crowd cheered as the spotlight found me. "She thought it was the tequila." Laughter rippled through the audience. "But I knew. I'd known since high school that she was it for me. I just needed her to catch up to my data set."

"Nerd," Justice coughed into his mic, earning more laughs.

"Says the man who cried at our vow renewal," Sam shot back before turning back to me. "Anyway, my beautiful, organizational wizard of a wife made me promise not to do anything spontaneous tonight."

I narrowed my eyes at him. "Sam..."

"But..." His grin was wicked as he gestured to the screen behind the stage. "She never said anything about planned spontaneity."

The screen lit up with a PowerPoint slide:

A COMPREHENSIVE ANALYSIS OF WHY SAMUEL DOGG CONTINUES TO FALL MORE IN LOVE WITH FAYE MOYO
YEAR ONE PERFORMANCE REVIEW

"Ten seconds!"

Tears burned my eyes as Sam walked to the edge of the stage, holding out his hand just like last year.

"Nine!"

"What do you say, love?" His eyes sparkled. "Want to help me present my findings?"

"Eight!"

"You made a PowerPoint?"

"Seven!"

"With graphs and everything."

"Six!"

"Color-coded?"

"Five!"

"Of course." His smile was soft. "I learned from the best."

"Four!"

I took his hand, letting him pull me into the lights.

"Three!"

"I love you," I whispered as his arm wrapped around my waist.

"Two!"

"I know." His forehead touched mine. "I have the statistical evidence to prove it."

"ONE!"

As fireworks burst overhead and the crowd erupted in cheers, I kissed my husband—planned and perfect and everything I never knew I needed.

Because sometimes the best forms of control...

Are knowing exactly when to let go.

"Happy Anniversary, my brown-eyed girl," Sam murmured against my lips.

And for once, I didn't need a PowerPoint to know exactly where this was going.

Though I had one prepared anyway.

Just in case.

**Thank you for reading Faye and Sam's story!
Want more Sam and Faye?**

Check out the bonus on my website at
EvieMitchell.com

Want all the stories in the Dogg Pack?
Visit my website and use the code EBOOK10
to get 10% off your next read!

ABOUT THE AUTHOR

Hey, I'm Evie Mitchell.
I'm a thirty-something romance author
(she/her/hers) living with disability. I believe in
inclusion, accessibility, and fierce romance. My
loves include steamy romance novels, my sexy
husband, our THREE sausage dogs (THE
FUR!!!), and my ever-growing collection of
book-related mugs.

As a woman with a diverse work history,
including in areas such as hospitality, retail,
emergency response, event management,
human rights, disability access, and security—
my books are filled with true stories
(bridezillas), worst-case scenarios
(malfunctioning zippers), and my favorite
tropes (one-bed).

I'm a strong proponent of #OwnVoices, and
specialize in fiercely inclusive happily ever
afters.

EvieMitchell.com
Socials: @EvieMitchellAuthor

ALSO BY EVIE MITCHELL

All Access Series

Knot My Type

Love Flushed

Darn Knit All

Common Scents

Larsson Siblings

Thunder Thighs

Clean Sweep

The X-List

Reality Check

The Christmas Contract

The A-List

Capricorn Cove

The Shake-up

Double the D

Muffin Top

The Mrs. Clause

New Year, Knew You

Double Breasted

As You Wish

You Sleigh Me

Meat Load

Resolution Revolution

Dogg Pack

Puppy Love

Bad English

The Frock Up

Pier Pressure

Trick or Trent

Reigning Hearts

The Marriage Claim

Silent Knight

Men of Trinity Bay

Kink in the Road

Nameless Souls MC

Runner

Wrath

Ghost

Shield

Elliot Security

Rough Edge
Bleeding Edge